LOVE POTION

#666

Nathan D. Ludwig

GENREBLAST
BOOKS

Previous edition edited by Patrick C. Harrison III

Second edition edited by Nathan D. Ludwig

Cover art and design by Jorge Iracheta

Interior layout and design by Will (@tlmason) on Fiverr

Also available from GenreBlast Books:

The Comfy-Cozy Nihilist: A Handbook of Dark Fiction by Nathan D. Ludwig
Devil Won't Let Me Be by Chad Farmer
Midnight Maniacs Vol. 1 by Chad Farmer & Nathan D. Ludwig

Praise for *Love Potion #666*

"A rollicking journey that carries all the fun of a hit grindhouse novel. Ludwig knows how to keep readers entertained!"

- Samantha Kolesnik, author of *True Crime* and *Waif*

"Great plot, great characters, great dialogue (to be expected from Nathan) and everyone knows how much I love a good one-liner. Plenty of them here to entertain, all wrapped up with a nasty grindhouse feel to proceedings."

- Mark Towse, author of *Nana* and *Crows*

"This is the second work I have read by Nathan, and it didn't disappoint. It is so hard to describe his style and work. But if you like absolute chaos, humor, and gore, this needs to skyrocket to the top of your reading list."

- E.C. Hanson, author of *Wicked Blood* and *Fake Somebodies, Real Nobodies*

Ludwig has a talent for fast paced, in your face writing. Especially of note is his use of the dirty simile -- kinda like a Raymond Chandler or Dashiel Hammett from hell.

- C.I.I. Jones, author of *A Boy and His Dog* and *If God Said, "Oi!"*

"Get ready for a ride that will leave you disgusted and laughing in the end!"

- Chad Farmer, author of *Devil Won't Let Me Be* and *Earth Truckers are Easy*

"I didn't know what to expect from this book by Nathan D. Ludwig. I went in blind, but soon found myself craving the next page time and again. Ludwig has written one hell of a debut."

- Terry Miller, author of *Den of the Wererats* and *Love You to Death*

"Every page progresses the story to an explosive climax I did not see coming. It's gory, funny, fast-paced, intelligently done, and has some of the best dialogue. Definitely recommend!"

- R.J. Benetti, author of *The Slappening* and *Santa Muerte Claus*

Praise for The Comfy-Cozy Nihilist:
A Handbook of Dark Fiction
Now Available from GenreBlast Books

"A gloriously twisted collection of stories that will make readers grimace, shoot steam from their ears, hold their rumbling guts, and think."

- Brennan LaFaro, author of *Noose* and *Slattery Falls*

"The Comfy-Cozy Nihilist is a great collection of short stories that entertains, makes you laugh, and then sucker punches you when you aren't looking."

- Mark MJ Green, author of *Abortus* and *Birdsong*

"This collection of dark stories was such a fun read. The perfect blend of humor and horror, each story left you feeling amused and uncomfortable but also satisfied with what you read."

- D.A. Latham, author of *Compulsions* and
You Should Have Let Me In

"This is a fantastically deranged collection of dark fiction. Chock full of eye-popping imagery and memorable moments of pure WTF! I really enjoy Ludwig's "voice"- his demented sense of humor."

- Evan Baughfman, author of *Vanishing of*
the 7th Grade* and *Bad For Your Teeth

"This book is a lovely cornucopia of dark tales with something delectable for every palette. Nathan Ludwig is a gifted writer who crafts stories that will either make you laugh with his take on life's absurdities or creep under your skin and stay there for some time."

- **Paul Grammatico, author of *Insects of the Damned* and *Starvation Lake***

"You will be hard pressed to find a better collection out right now. This is a banger from the first story to the last."

- **Christina Pfeiffer, reviewer for Mothers of Mayhem & Uncomfortably Dark and author of *Cooter***

For Chad Douglas Farmer, a true brother.
The only person I know who would willingly watch
A Serbian Film with me.
Twice.

ACKNOWLEDGEMENTS

Thank you to Chad Farmer, Samantha Kolesnik, Mike Lombardo, Jeff Frumess, Jeremy Herbert, and Zane Hershberger for being cool, genuine, and supportive friends.

Thanks to the reviewers out there spotlighting indie horror and genre fiction. Your hard work is appreciated.

Special shout out to the original cast of the short film *Dead of Night*: Sandra Doolittle, Suzette Vieu, Tim Vester, Andrew Mayhill & Josh Johnson. They're the ones that first brought Teena, Leanna, Wallis, Ronnie, and Mikey to bloody life.

AUTHOR'S NOTE

I f this second edition of *Love Potion #666* were a DVD or a Blu-Ray of a movie, you might call it the special edition or the director's cut or something of the sort. Maybe the extended cut. I'm not calling it the Author's Preferred Edition or anything like that as I feel it would come across as disingenuous and reductive to the first edition and the readers who supported that release. I'm very proud of the version that came out through D&T Publishing but over the last two years or so I developed an unquenchable hankering to do another edition that will hopefully end up as the last word on this book for a very, very long time. Probably forever.

What's new? Well, if you've already read *Love Potion #666*, you've read the story as it was intended. If you're looking to revisit it, then this is absolutely the preferred edition to do so. The happenings at Fanny's Hot Box have been expanded a lot. There's more violence, gore, and sex all around. You'll spot a few more character details and interactions. It feels more fleshed out but with the same crazy characters and snappy dialogue. Some typos have been identified and fixed. The story itself has not been altered in any drastic way. Except for the ending, maybe.

If we were firmly in 2005, this would be the Killer Cut or the Xtreme Edition. You get the idea.

Bon Appetit. See you at the Cluck Shack!

Best,
Nathan D. Ludwig

2/25/24

"Poisonous lookalike
Little Miss Gun-to-a-Knife fight
Poisonous lookalike
What're you trying to do?"

- Warren Zevon,
"Poisonous Lookalike" (1995)

"Shut that cunt's mouth or I'll come over there
and fuck-start her head."

- *The Way of the Gun* (2000)

Table of Contents

Author's Note... xiii

Prologue 1

Part One: A No Good, Low-Down, Dirty, Backstabbing Bitch ... 2

    One... 5

    Two.. 10

    Three.. 13

    Four.. 16

    Five.. 19

    Six... 21

    Seven... 29

Part Two: Bring Out Your Dead 34

    Eight.. 37

    Nine... 43

    Ten... 48

    Eleven... 52

    Twelve... 55

    Thirteen... 59

    Fourteen... 64

    Fifteen... 68

    Sixteen.. 70

    Seventeen... 74

    Eighteen... 77

    Nineteen... 86

Part Three: Road Games... 92

    Twenty.. 94

    Twenty-One... 98

Twenty-Two... 104

Twenty-Three... 106

Twenty-Four... 111

Twenty-Five.. 115

Twenty-Six... 126

Twenty-Seven... 129

Twenty-Eight... 132

Twenty-Nine... 134

Thirty.. 137

Thirty-One... 143

Thirty-Two... 155

Thirty-Three... 167

Thirty-Four... 169

Thirty-Five.. 174

Thirty-Six... 186

Part Four: The Inevitable Death Of Leanna Forsythe................ 188

Thirty-Seven.. 190

Thirty-Eight... 198

Thirty-Nine... 202

Forty.. 208

Forty-One... 215

Forty-Two... 219

Forty-Three... 221

Forty-Four... 224

Forty-Five... 246

Epilogue 250

About The Author 256

PROLOGUE

Leanna Simone Forsythe was born on a Monday. December the 14th, to be exact, to Teena Lisbeth Forsythe (née Collins) and Derek Michael Forsythe in room 248 of the Corpus Christi Memorial Hospital. A healthy eight pounds and four ounces. The delivery itself was unremarkable other than the usual grunting and screaming.

No storms, no snow, no portents. Just a slight touch of unseasonable warmth. Nearly seventy degrees Fahrenheit. Mild. Pleasant. Forgettable.

The nurse brought fried chicken, corn on the cob, and mashed potatoes for their first meal as parents. It had been sitting out for several minutes before they brought it, so the warmth was but a shadow of the immediate past.

As they all dozed sporadically, Teena was sure she heard another expectant mother get wheeled in and deliver her own bundle in the span of forty-five minutes. Either a wide-eyed teenager or a Catholic shut-in wife on her eighth kid. Never in-between. Was that what true love was like? Hopping out double time for your dear old mother?

Leanna didn't cry much that first night. She did, however, stare back at Teena with unblinking eyes. Teena was too tired to be unnerved, but she noted it.

Derek was overjoyed to have a cute, quiet baby.

Teena knew better.

1

PART ONE

A NO GOOD, LOW-DOWN, DIRTY, BACKSTABBING BITCH

Dear Fucking Diary,

So here I am. All vulnerable and shit. Doctor Fuckface McHandsypants says this is supposed to help with my anger. A coping mechanism. Whatever the fuck that means. It wasn't enough that I agreed to do this horseshit, but now I need to recall past traumas in order to assign the proper perspective when it comes to the disproportionate amount of animosity I have for my mother. His words, not mine. He ain't wrong, though. Bitch can rot in hell for all I care. Can't keep her hands off my men, so I can't keep mine off hers. All's fair. As for past traumas or whatever, I know what really happened to Dad. She doesn't think I do. But I do. At least I feel it. She thinks just because I was five I don't remember it. But I do. I remember how I felt. Scared as shit. Confused. Oh, I remember that night. She said he just left one day. Left my ass. I never saw him leave. I don't care how old I was or wasn't, I'd remember something like that. He was just gone. But he didn't leave. You get what I mean? She thinks she's so fucking smart. All the spell books and voodoo rituals in the world ain't gonna fix what we got between us. Bad blood don't fix right. Ever.

So here's to the first of many of these fuckshit journal entries. I think I'm kinda getting used to it now. Sharing and shit. Honestly, I don't give a fuck if anyone sees this. If the doc thinks I'm embarrassed to show this, he ain't seen nothing yet. That's what he gets for thinking he can jerk off in front of me and get away with it. That motherfucker's future self is in for some past traumas. Maybe then they'll take me seriously and realize I ain't fucking around. Oh, I got a plan. I got a real good plan. I just need that bitch out of the country while I'm not locked up. Timing is everything. Know what I mean? Anyway, Ronnie'll be here any minute. Maybe he'll take my mind off her. God knows I need it.

-LF

ONE...

Now that she was out, it was time to pay the world back. And Teena.

For everything.

Stupid fucking bitch. Waste of fucking time. What the fuck is she looking at in that folder?

If looks could actually, instantly kill, Leanna Forsythe would be the world's most notorious flash mass murderer by a bloody landslide.

Just sitting in that old crimson crushed velvet armchair in that ancient office, arms folded and eyes locked on Miss Chalmers, laser beams of death and judgment seemed to emanate from her pupils like whip-cracked tendrils, utterly devastating any who came into contact with them.

Except Miss Evelyn Chalmers, a woman who had seen and heard it all before. Even from Leanna, a veritable bottomless cesspool of sailor language and medieval manners. None of it seemed to phase Chalmers. It was as if shocking deeds and words just made her tired. So very tired.

The austere, middle-aged woman peered over her glasses and down onto the involuntarily leering Leanna with all the interest of a dog show judge trying slightly more than the bare minimum to give a fuck about this year's second place pooch.

"And how are we today, Miss Forsythe?" Chalmers thumbed through Leanna's manila file folder with the exact opposite of zest.

"Peachy. Just peachy. Like a fucking peach." If Taylor Swift had a twenty-three-year-old doppelganger with a penchant for larceny and sodomy, it would be Leanna Fucking Forsythe.

"I won't miss that," Miss Chalmers mused with nary a squint of emotion.

Leanna flicked her eyes around the room in response to the comatose social worker's retort. The place resembled the skin casing of a corpse that died on the set of Captain Kangaroo followed by someone vomiting the entire decade of the 1980s on top of it in hopes that would fix the problem. There had to be some secret rule about public service buildings not being allowed to update their decor without a goddamn act of Congress.

Especially halfway houses. Especially the Chalmers-Faveshim Halfway Home for Young Women. The place reeked of disappointment, depression, and dreams that energetically committed suicide. The smell was a lot like old leather and stale perfume. Sad perfume.

That would be her brand of perfume she'd sell if she ever got out of this fucking exit interview. Sad. By Leanna. *The only woman you'll need to impress is yourself. And that's only when you feel like it. Sad.*

"That it?" Her strawberry blonde hair seemed to bristle with disgust as she uncrossed her arms and immediately crossed her legs.

"Excited?" Chalmers closed the file folder on Leanna with brisk indifference. The breeze wafted right onto Leanna's increasingly impatient face.

"What does it look like?"

"Do you have a ride? We can provide—"

"I can walk."

"I didn't ask if you could walk, I—"

"I'm not a fucking cripple. Fresh air and shit."

Chalmers launched into her fully memorized and obligatory *fuck off* spiel. "Your parole officer is Marion Killford. You'll meet with her every Friday, but I advise you get in touch with her as soon as possible. She's not the type to keep waiting."

Her glowing appraisal of Killford made Leanna chuckle a puff of hot breath through her nose. "Or it's back to here, right?"

"Or it's back to prison, Leanna. I don't know what strings were pulled to get you such an early release, but this is it for you. No more unlicensed firearms and no more dealing ecstasy to minors would be words to the wise. Are you going to be wise?"

"Anything else?"

"Refraining from sodomizing public servants would also be wise."

And that right there made Leanna smile wider than a twelve-lane freeway on the prairie. "Thought so."

"And I would also advise you to stay away from Michael Rundgren. And his gun collection." Chalmers made it a point to wag her finger right at the mention of Mikey's name. Trying to keep the evil peanut butter from melding with the gullible yet dangerous jelly. Gullible grape jelly.

"Mikey? He ain't nothin' scary."

"It isn't him that has people scared, Miss Forsythe."

Leanna chuckled with her mouth closed as she stood up.

7

Miss Chalmers handed Leanna two business cards. "Here's Killford's number. I recommend calling her as soon as possible. And there's my number. If you ever need anything."

"Like what?" Leanna barely studied either card before shoving them down her shirt, never unlocking eyes with Chalmers for even a second.

"Well, anything. Guidance, advice, questions you might—"

"Tips on how to groom my pussy?"

"There's that thing I won't miss again." It looked as if Chalmers pursed her lips harder than anyone had pursed lips in human history, but it didn't actually happen. At least outwardly. Not all the way.

Miss Chalmers then just got up and extended her hand to Leanna with certainty. It almost felt like a condescending gesture to Leanna, who stared at it, indifferent. Like a sociopath studying an earnest toddler.

"Well, I suppose that's the long and short of it. Good luck, Miss Forsythe."

"Sure." Leanna headed for the door without shaking her hand.

"Oh, one more thing."

Leanna stopped short without turning to look back, hiding her tightening, rictus frown from Chalmers.

"Where are you planning on staying? Hopefully not with Mr. Rundgren. That would be most unwise." That sounded as if Chalmers almost gave a shit. *The fuck was that all about?*

"I was hoping to shack up with you. That okay?" She wanted to sound like she was joking, but it came out as a guttural threat, like most of her humor.

Miss Chalmers' expression made it seem as if she absolutely couldn't tell if Leanna was joking, so she just softly sounded out the worst possible question to ask her.

"What about your mother?"

Leanna finally turned to look back at Miss Chalmers with an awful, hateful stare of deadly death.

"What about her?"

For any normal person, that question would usually sound like a mild inquisition. Maybe passive aggressive signaling at worst. But from Leanna's mouth and face, it was a vocal harbinger of doom.

Chalmers involuntarily took a step back from her own desk upon witnessing Leanna's gorgon-esque scowl. She snapped her eyes shut as Leanna slammed the door on her way out.

A sigh of relief escaped her at the realization the girl was gone. For now.

TWO...

Hector didn't *look* dead. At least not to Teena.

He was dead, though. Mama Francine announced he had indeed expired. Much to the village's wailing chagrin, he was the very definition of the term. He lay motionless on a stone slab amidst hundreds of Haitian villagers. Arms crossed, decorated in face paint, chicken feathers and animal blood all over him. Still, but with a slight smile fixed to his weathered face.

There was lots of chanting and singing all around as his friends and family celebrated his life and consoled each other. It reached a fever pitch as a regal woman stepped out of the crowd. Mama Francine. Stout, with kind eyes and pock-marked skin. Dressed in full voodoo mambo priestess robes. She stretched her arms out wide and shook them vigorously a few times. The crowd died down to complete silence.

One person in the throng looked markedly out of place: a pale woman with wide eyes, a sad face, and simple black robes. Teena Forsythe. Creeping through the end of her late forties, she had a worn and weary beauty about her. The kind that's unnoticed upon first glance, but desired more and more with each successive encounter. Her thick, wild auburn hair accentuated her pronounced cheekbones and provided a contrast to her full, yet blanched, pink lips.

Teena remembered meeting Hector on her last visit. How cheerful and noncommittal he was. Nothing seemed to bother him. Except dying. She remembered distinctly him saying he had a fear of dying. When she asked him why, he hesitated to answer before changing the subject altogether.

Mama Francine moved to speak, and the crowd prepared to drape themselves over her every word.

"Hector was *us*."

The crowd buzzed and hummed in approval.

"He represented us. Understood us. We understood him."

Teena tried to move up closer to her through the overflowing crowd as the priestess continued.

"As old and wise as he was, he still feared death. Death. It's not his fault, of course. Death follows us all. Especially around here. But Hector had a sickness of death. He was terrified of it. Like something waited for him on the other side. He wanted to remain here. Forever."

Mama Francine went silent for a moment, scanning the crowd. She locked eyes with Teena, who smiled slightly.

"And who would argue with him? Hector was the kindest, most generous man any of us knew. Having him around forever wouldn't be so bad now, right?" A smattering of laughter from the crowd as heads nodded in approval. "Tonight we are going to give Hector what he wanted, to keep death away. He's out there right now, waiting for us to reconnect his soul with his body. Shall we honor him?"

A roar of approval swelled and popped from the crowd as Teena remained hypnotized with wonder and excitement. Mama

Francine pulled an old purple velvet bag from her robes and lifted it high with a victorious grin.

"We will bring him back to us!"

The crowd chanted "*Oui!*" in approval several times. Mama Francine opened the bag and poured the contents onto Hector's body. It was a purplish, smoky dust. She dumped the last of it into his mouth and then closed it with a gentle nudge of her fingers. She brought her hands just inches away from Hector and glided them up and down his body, as if some unseen force kept her from actually touching him.

The crowd mumbled something in French, gradually getting louder and louder as Mama Francine joined in. It all reached critical mass as the noise became unbearable. Teena looked all around her, worry and anxiety now replacing her wonder and excitement. And then it all stopped. An awful silence coated the night as all waited for something to happen.

Hector coughed. Some in the crowd applauded. Others gasped. Some remained silent. Mama Francine clapped triumphantly. Hector shook all over roughly and coughed some more. She helped him sit up straight, patting his back. A mother nurturing a sick child.

"He has returned!"

Teena applauded feverishly, even laughing a little bit. *She's so good at this. Makes it look easy.*

Mama Francine glanced at her again as she helped up Hector. Did she just nod slightly at Teena?

Yes. Yes, she did.

Right then and there Teena swore to herself she would never tell Mama Francine that she'd seen this all before somewhere else.

THREE...

Corpus Christi reeked of a dirty toilet baked in french fry grease this time of year. It was all Leanna could do not to smoke her entire pack of cigs at once to stave off the enslaving odor of the Gulf Coast.

They didn't start off as *her* cigs. But Lucretia didn't mind handing them over at all. You don't need hands to palm a pack of cigs and a sweet vintage zippo when you're busy holding your gushing, broken nose in place. That's what that bitch gets for threatening to rape Mikey when she gets out. As if she'll ever get out of there.

There being the Chalmers-Faveshim Halfway Home for Young Women. It used to be Wayward Women, but that kind of impersonal turn-of-the-twentieth-century verbiage went out of style in a huff recently. At least that was what Leanna heard. She heard a lot of things inside. Like how Teena was in Haiti. Still.

Good. Bitch won't know what hit her when she gets back.

Her meager belongings in a few bags on the ground next to her, she leaned flippantly against the old wood-carved sign for her most recent prison as she lit up one of Lucretia's cigs with Lucretia's Zippo.

My Zippo now, bitch.

Before she had any more time to plot against her mother, a beat-up Chevy Impala pulled up in front of her, 80s new wave blaring out the windows. Leanna tossed her cigarette and approached the driver's window. The music went low, the window rolled down and a trim and built woman in her early forties with a young boy's haircut popped her head out. Marion C. Killford. Her Crocodile polo shirt looked in need of an industrial iron. A voice akin to a sugar-free smack in the ear.

"You Forsythe?"

"Leanna's fine, sir."

"Get in before I change my mind."

Leanna grabbed her shit and scooted into the backseat, mumbling something most certainly vulgar to herself all the while.

Killford sped off like she was late for something other than picking up Leanna from a life of state-monitored drudgery.

~666~

The inside of her on-life-support Impala smelled similar to your Irish grandpa dying while taking a shit in a burning cigarette factory. In 1968.

"Uh, thanks for the pickup. Not a lot of options around here." Was that civility in Leanna's tone? Must have been a fucking mistake.

"Yeah, heard all about you."

"Like what?" Leanna caught Killford leering at her through her sunglasses in the rearview mirror.

Killford didn't even flinch. "Heard you're a real rock star."

"Everything you heard about me is true."

Killford returned her eyes to the road, breaking her poker face. "So you reformed now?"

"Haven't decided yet."

"Well, I hope for your sake you are. I'd hate to see you go to waste back in the big house."

"The fuck's that supposed to—"

"You like Prefab Sprout?"

Before Leanna could answer, as if it mattered, Killford blared the music again and hit the gas.

FOUR...

The interior of Teena's hut looked almost exactly like she felt. Worn out and slightly sick of it all. And that was just the walls. The dirt floor had an old, patterned carpet in the middle, attempting to throw people off the fact that it was a carpet on top of a dirt fucking floor. Teena could not stop staring at it. She felt like that carpet more days than not. It whispered of a dynamic triangular pattern once proudly displayed all over it. Now worn to nothing. Even that reminded Teena of herself.

Her cot was less entrancing. Soldiers in the Korean War had softer accommodations. But it was a place to stay and some in the village didn't even have that. Teena tried to give her hut to one of the mothers on the outskirts when she visited the first time. Mama Francine refused to allow such a thing. Teena never saw that mother again. After her second visit, she stopped offering things to people. Something told her they would not take it anyway. They were afraid of Mama. Teena wasn't but she understood why others might be.

Mama Francine silently glided in as Teena stared at that damn dirt-covering carpet, pretending to be deep in thought. Anything to keep her mind off what awaited her back home.

"There's a difference between meditating and obsession, dearie." Mama Francine reached out a hand to Teena as she sat down next to her.

Teena broke her carpet trance and smiled softly at her. They embraced, but Teena slunk away from her shortly thereafter. Mama Francine noticed but pressed on.

"I hope I didn't frighten you with our little ceremony last night."

Teena laughed a little too hard in defense. "Oh no, of course not, I—"

"Sometimes those things can drive someone like you away. But I took a chance to see if you had the nerve. And you did. You really did."

Remembering the sublime insanity of seeing a resurrection in person again, Teena's eyes lit up involuntarily. "It was...amazing. Even more than what I thought it would be."

"You haven't—"

"What?"

"You haven't already tried it on your own, have you?"

"What? Why would you... I would never—"

Mama Francine smiled nervously, leaning in closer to Teena. "Good. You don't need to be messing with such things just yet. Trying to reconnect the spirit to the body after more than a few days is a recipe for misery. Trust me, I would know."

Teena nodded like a child tolerating a lecture from a parent.

Mama Francine clapped her hands together, signaling her way of changing the subject altogether. "Are you ready for your couché tonight?"

Teena looked back at the carpet again. Her spirit animal. "I don't know if ready's the word, but I'll meet it head on. There's nothing else for me now."

Mama placed her hands on Teena's shoulders, very parent-like. "That's as good an answer as anyone's ever given me. Just remember why you're here and everything else will come naturally."

They hugged again in an almost unnecessarily tight embrace.

"Thank you, Mama. I don't know where I would be without you. I mean that."

In Corpus blasted Christi. With her.

Mama nodded with all the wisdom of a thousand-year-old sage. "I know, dearie. I know."

If you only knew. If you only really, really knew. That would be swell.

FIVE...

Leanna's bedroom remained more-or-less the way she left it before she went to prison. Metal band posters mixed with disaster articles from random newspaper headlines were plastered to the wall. A mix of black and neon pinks and purples jousted with each other for identity all over the place. A ragged teddy bear was placed neatly on the still-made bed, waiting patiently for its owner to return.

The door to her bathroom creaked open as a toilet flushed weakly. Out stepped twenty-eight-year-old local lothario Ronnie McGiffin. Exuding equal parts confidence and laziness, he yawned heartily and adjusted his crotch as he shuffled over to the bed and plopped down. He pulled out his phone and dialed a number. Some waiting and eye-rolling before he was forced to leave a voicemail.

"Hey, babe. Just checking to see if you're on your way yet. You know I'm not good with time zones. Anyway, just call me back when you get a chance. Still at your place. Think I'll hang here until you get back. Love you. Bye."

After a moment of attempted deep thought, he tossed his phone behind him carelessly and headed over to the aging desktop PC in the corner of the room. He slid down in front of it and checked something quickly. Still connected to the internet. Score.

With the same excitement level as if he were voting for city council, Ronnie undid his pants and pulled them down to his ankles along with his boxers. He put his belt around his neck and notched it tight with one hand as he searched for something to fit his current mood. Horses? Midgets? Both?

He eventually found something to hang his hat (or belt) on with a site plainly titled Horses Who Love Midgets. No fancy wordplay; just earnest advertising. Without much enthusiasm, he masturbated with one hand and choked himself with his belt in the other hand. He was soon so into his new favorite website that he didn't even hear the sound of a shitty, lecherous Impala halfheartedly approaching the house.

SIX...

The Forsythe residence lay silent and still, waiting for someone to come back and breathe life into it again. With Teena being gone so long, the yard was in serious need of trimming and a Mount Everest of newspapers and junk flyers made its home ignorantly on the doorstep. The house itself was a modest rambler out in the boonies, the paint job ignored for years, gutters askew. The usual external issues signifying the human disarray within.

Killford's car pulled up halfway through the circular driveway, as close to the door as she could get. It was so unforgivingly dark out there that she flicked the high beams on just to be able to see their surroundings.

"I bet you don't get Mormon hucksters out here." She sounded proud of her attempt at humor.

Leanna treated it as a serious question. "Have you ever met a missionary? Their cardio is supernatural."

"You sure you don't wanna go nowhere else?"

"Where?"

"How 'bout my house?"

Killford's offer was considered for all of about two seconds before Leanna sighed, cocked her head, and slid out of the backseat, slamming the passenger door. As she slung her bags over her shoulder, Killford got a great look at her ass. When Leanna turned back around, she barely hid her gaze.

"Right then. Make sure you check in on—"

"Friday. Got it. Anything else?"

"Yeah. Don't break the law. Or I'll take pleasure in breaking you."

"That a come-on or a suicide pact?"

"Both."

Killford sped off, blaring her music loud as can be. Gravel sprayed out every which way, threatening to pelt Leanna with bits of home. *Welcome back, bitch.*

"What a twat."

Leanna was left alone in the dead of night. The house seemed to leer at her like a pervert uncle you only see at family functions where the food is free.

As she stared back into the abyss of the blackened abode, she rubbed her hands together with sinister vigor. The most sadistic Mr. Miyagi impersonator to ever live.

Time to get down to fucking business.

~666~

Leanna stood in the empty dark of the doorway to the house, pocketknife still in hand. It was painfully easy to pick the lock. Was it a trap? Or was Leanna just lucky enough to catch her unawares? No preparation before she left on her long trip? Was Teena slipping? It was too much to process right now.

Her shifting eyes scanned the room she now inhabited. Her most hated room in the whole house. Figures. Nothing's changed here.

About five years ago, Teena insisted on making the living room - the front fucking room of the whole fucking house - her personal voodoo lab/museum. Leanna's shrill objections to this went over like a lead balloon on Jupiter.

Animal fetishes, shrunken heads, jars, and vials of mammal fetuses (including humans), ceremonial and sacrificial knives, all manner of blood samples. All the occult hits were present. There was even a whole collection of urns containing human remains. Teena once joked to Leanna that they were all that was left of her long-ago teenage romances. Leanna never laughed because she knew about that whole 'much truth spoken in jest' thingy all too well. It was a Jeopardy answer that stuck with her for some weird reason.

And the books. The goddamned books. Books out the wazoo's wazoo's wazoo. Leanna tried to read some of them, but she soon grew to hate the grotesque drawings and sketches found within them. And the pages smelled biological in nature. She asked her mother – politely for a change – to do something with at least the books. Put them in the shed. Or her bedroom. Anything but the living room. She distinctly remembered her mom snorting an invidious laugh at that request and then going out on a date minutes later with a man she met at a swap meet two days before.

Classic Teena.

It almost all looked refined in the darkness. But it was time to face reality.

Leanna fumbled around, reaching for a light switch. She found one with a swiping paw and squinted as the brightness overwhelmed her. She scanned the accursed room for something specific, but her full attention was soon attracted elsewhere.

A faint noise down the hall. Like a repeated smacking sound.

She turned to look down the long, dark hallway and saw a light oozing from underneath the door at the opposite end.

Holy shit. Could it be that easy?

Leanna snuck down the hall, old tennis shoes making zero noise on the ancient shag carpet. Her disgusted frown blossomed as she got closer, the sounds much more pronounced. Skin-on-skin friction. The sound of leather squeezing tightly. Loud moaning. Both men and women. And...horses?

Do horses moan? What the fuck?

She placed a hand on the knob slower than she'd ever placed her hand on anything in her life, perishing the thought of ruining this gift of an ambush. Locked, but she knew her own door better than she knew the ins and outs of the Corpus Christi Corrections Department. Leanna kicked it in with muscular zeal and it burst open with a swift, hard CRRRACK!

And then she saw him.

Goddamned Ronnie McGiffin.

Her face turned the color of the planet Mars if it had a menstrual cycle. "You fucking motherfucker." She knew *exactly* what had to happen to this actual fucker of mothers.

Ronnie, pants down and in mid-strangulation - blushed-out and bloodshot eyes - gasped as he let go of the belt. "L-Leanna, I... You're not supposed to be out till... What the fuck?!"

"Good behavior, you piece of shit!" Leanna charged at Ronnie, shoulder out, knocking him off his chair. She snatched the belt still around his neck, pulling as hatefully hard as she could. Ronnie grabbed for it desperately, clawing at his neck. He ripped chunks of skin off in a dying panic, blood spattering onto his lime green polo shirt in weak spurts. Losing consciousness by the nanosecond.

In that moment, Leanna became a shaved wolverine of smeared-lipstick rage and gourmet violence as she forced the life out of her former lover. "Didn't think you'd see me again, huh, bitch? She ain't here to protect you now, you backstabbing cuntfuck!"

Ronnie had only seen Leanna this angry before once. Just once. It was just after he suggested that a threesome with the two of them and Teena would bring them all closer together. He now most likely regretted that decision. Amongst other things, of course.

As if sensing his very last thought, Leanna pulled even harder, making her just as purple as Ronnie. Except Ronnie was now a deep violet.

"...Leee—"

"Fuck..."

She pulled with all her remaining strength, knuckles bleaching at her titanic effort.

"...you!"

She snapped his neck like an annoying stalk of undernourished celery. His left eye burst a blood vessel, his right eye just plain left his head with a sucking pop, and a sickening sound of air escaped his clenched mouth as a smashed accordion of a whine. A defective whoopee cushion no one would ever play with again.

Leanna attempted to catch her breath, straddled punishingly over Ronnie. She looked like she'd just climaxed as her bosom heaved hard and fast. The spoils of good behavior and early release were starting to pile up.

That felt so fucking good.

~666~

Back in the front room, Leanna wandered amongst all the odd and weird stuff, scanning for something specific with her bloodshot viper eyes. An old cupboard in the corner caught her eye. She rushed over and flung it open carelessly, rummaging through old jars and urns willy-nilly.

A particular urn fell out of the cupboard and hit the ground with a smash. Dust billowed every which way. Leanna coughed for a spell before reaching for a broom leaning on the wall.

"Bitch should'a rode this to Haiti."

Leanna swept the ash and broken urn pieces underneath the cupboard haphazardly. Clearing her eyes, she looked around for something else and spotted an old hope chest half-covered by a moth-eaten blanket in the other corner. She swooped over and tried to open it. Locked. She screamed in face-punching, vehicular homicide frustration, pulling at her hair and smacking herself repeatedly. After some rapid breathing, she calmed down as much as possible and counted to ten slowly, methodically. *Vengefully.*

She grabbed her pocketknife and wiggled it around in the lock. After some rough fidgeting, she picked it clean and threw the lid wide open. Wider than her contempt for her mother. Inside, all manner of curios. Old pictures, tied-up pouches, locks of hair, little bones. So on and so forth. Leanna spotted a polaroid of a handsome bearded man in his thirties.

Dad?

After a brief moment, she recognized him fully and caressed the picture surprisingly gently.

Dad...

Try as she might, Teena could not suppress Leanna's core memories of her father. They were all there, even if they weren't tangible, dredge-worthy memories. Some were just smells. Others were just sounds. And others still were just feelings. His laugh. Her own laugh when he told a joke or broke out the tickles. How he smelled after a long day of work. The scents from the kitchen when dinner was ready courtesy of Daddy. Even the unpleasant emanations of the arguments between him and her mother were broken down into positive morsels. The way he fought, the way he argued with her was eloquent. Measured. Calm. At least that's how she recalled it. The negative stuff didn't survive the trip to Leanna's adulthood remembrances. And here was yet more proof of Teena's anti-paternal skullduggery. Holding out on vintage photos. It even smelled like him. What the fuck was she trying to do? Short of a lobotomy, Teena would never win that fight as long as Leanna had something to say about it.

I got you, Dad. She can't hurt you anymore. Fuck that chest.

She tucked the photo in her frayed jean shorts and continued to rummage through the chest. Underneath the top layer of stuff she revealed what she was really looking for. Several velvet purple pouches tied nice and tight with gold string. She ripped one open and sniffed mannishly. This was it. The love dust. They were right in front of her after all these years. Teena didn't even bother to hide them in a different spot. Unbelievable. A wicked, Grinchy smile

27

crept across her face as she grabbed every single pouch, around a dozen in all.

She slammed the lid shut, failing to contain her unbridled chortling.

Jackpot, you fucking bitch.

SEVEN...

P*lease just let me get through this night...*
Imprinted on the dirt floor in the fetal position, naked and covered in animal blood and feathers, Teena hoped and prayed this would be the answer to all her problems. Especially her.

That rug was nowhere to be seen. All the better for it. It wouldn't want to be a part of what's about to happen on that ground it once took for granted.

The mumbled chanting coming from just outside the hut was simultaneously soothing and alarming. She wanted to embrace it all and simply let it happen, but something small deep down inside of her was scared.

Terrified.

What if she wasn't ready for this? Would she die because of that? Maybe Mama Francine had planned such a thing all along. *Stupid white cow. How dare you come here to our home and presume to know anything about our way of life? An infatuation with death is no substitute for what we do here. What we really do. You know what we really do. Don't you, Teena?*

Before she could act on that morsel of fear, Teena convulsed from rapid fire muscle spasms all over her body, unable to stop it or slow it down. It took over her whole body, making her skull ache and her guts quiver. An inescapable urge flooded her very being and before she knew it, she was chanting right alongside the villagers just out of sight. Beyond any trance. More like an aggressive out-of-body experience where she could actually see a rotting corpse manipulating her muscles and voice while she watched helpless from afar.

A sucker punch of pain struck her mind's eye. Staggering, nigh unbearable. Made her eyes water as a guttural moan escaped her quivering mouth.

In her mind, she was forced to witness horrible, inescapable visions as if they were right in front of her.

Leanna stabbed with feral abandon at her with a bloody kitchen knife, screaming like a rabid animal all the while. Teena could feel every puncture, every slice. Blood spurted from her body as she gurgled a weakening protest of sadness and regret. Not an ounce of shock or surprise, though. Teena felt herself dying inside. Breath fading and ebbing. Eyes growing dim. But before she could feel that true death, she tumbled violently into another vision. She felt like she was about to puke. Puke where? In her mind? Was that even possible?

Before she could find out, a huge unlit pyre of dead, naked men stood before her beneath a purple-tinged black sky. No clouds. No horizon. Just the stillness of judgment and silent scorn. Bodies stacked higher than any human eye could comprehend. Their blood mingled and drained into a massive puddle at Teena's feet. One of the corpses stirred, causing the whole mass to shake and shift. She swore she could hear one of them mumble *"Teena"* to her underneath so many other shuddering bodies.

In a flash, she was in front of an unmarked grave in the middle of the woods. Something frightened her terribly, but she couldn't place it for certain. She could sense something moving amongst the trees. Walking on her nervous system. Watching her. Deciding on her very fate. She moved to leave, and a decayed hand burst through the ground and grabbed her ankle flesh, clawing greedily at it, shredding it to pieces.

Teena screamed the scream of sudden, agonizing death.

Oblivion. But also the sensation of experiencing oblivion. No sight, no sound, no speech. Trapped in a pit of darkness. She reached out for nothing in particular, aided by frantically blinking eyes that didn't work. Propelling a voice from her mouth with no sound. Trying to hear her own screams from ears that weren't there.

Eternity seemed to pass.

A gust of persistent force pushed her from the darkness to the light like forcing herself to wake from a dream repeatedly, only to wake into another dream.

Until Teena opened her eyes with a suffocated gasp.

Am I alive...?

...Do I deserve to be?

~666~

The villagers gathered outside. Hundreds of them, silently awaiting something to happen. Anything. Mama Francine was at the head of the crowd, an emotionless face leading the motionless charge, as it were. The anticipation as loud as it was quiet.

Teena ambled from the hut, shaking and muttering. She put on her simple black robe with vanquished hands and fingers, wiping blood from her blank face. The crowd seemed to take a massive breath before they applauded for Teena. For the strange, self-conscious woman they'd been told to love. Mama Francine quieted them down with barely a wave of her hand. It was all that was needed.

"What did you see?"

Teena scanned the gathering in front of her, frantically spent but awestruck.

"The future."

My future.

Mama Francine shrugged off her regal black-and-red fringed robe and nestled it around Teena with a loving smile.

"Welcome, mambo priestess. You are one of us now."

Teena cried tears of exhaustion and joy as the crowd congratulated her, patting her on the back, hugging her, shaking her hand. Wishing her well in French.

Did one of them just warn me?

With barely a second of thought on that, Teena spotted figures dancing in the distance. All around the outskirts of the village. Faceless forms dancing just for her, she assumed.

No. Writhing. Beckoning.

That small morsel of terror returned and expanded into a much bigger and harder to hide size.

It seemed as if the very realm of death itself had opened up to her. And she wasn't so sure she was a fan of that anymore.

Her disorientation refusing to abate, Teena stumbled away from the crowd and would have fallen straight to the ground if not for the supernatural reflexes of Mama Francine.

"I've got you, dearie."

Teena's paranoia from the dancing shapes materialized into a mutter of words.

"The things...out there...in the trees..."

Mama Francine smiled a smile that made Teena freeze inside her own body.

"You'll never stop seeing them. Just ask Hector."

Despite her nerve-burning fear, the taxing ceremony had proven too much for her to remain cogent. Teena let go of herself into a concrete-laden slumber of oblivion.

PART TWO
BRING OUT
YOUR DEAD

Dear Fucking Diary,

Well, now Ronnie's fucking my mom, too. How fucking far away from her do I have to get to be happy? What is her fucking problem? Doc McStiffens says it's her misguided way of trying to connect with me. Be close to me. If she wants to connect with me, she sure has a funny fucking way of showing it. I swear to God, if he lies to me about fucking her and doesn't come clean, I'm gonna kill him. I mean, I'm gonna kill her, too. Just not yet. And she knows I am. I think she's resigned herself to it. She actually apologized to me the other day. Apologized. For everything. And she ain't even said nothing about Wallis yet. At least nothing I remember. Does she know? I felt her staring at me when I was trying to go to sleep the other night. Like in the hallway, just looking at me. Right through the back of my fucking head. It made me anxious as all hell. I wanted to yell "What the fuck do you want?!" But I couldn't. I couldn't make noise come out of my mouth at all whatsoever. I don't wanna feel like that again. She said she's got something to talk to me about. About the living situation between us. Probably as in I need to start paying rent. Fuck that. She owes me for what she's done to me. Fucking treacherous bitch. There's no way she knows about what Mikey done for me. Ain't possible. He's the only one who'll never fuck around with her. Never. But I can't let it happen again.

Never again. I might be living in a new place next time I write one of these fucking things. Maybe with Mikey? Might be nice. I think she's watching me again. Staring at me behind my back while I write this. I think she's planning something too. But what? What the fuck is it? I hate surprises. Maybe doc will jerk off facing the corner this time instead of making me watch. I could use a break from that shit. Just once.

-LF

EIGHT...

Within South Central Corpus Christi lay the residential paradise known as Madrigal Winds Trailer Garden. Row after row of ramshackle, rattly, and overall failing mobile homes. Just left of center, next to the one painted Pepto pink, a rusty vagabond of a trailer tried to hide in plain sight amidst a sea of its shitty cousins in the least welcoming trailer park this side of redneck purgatory.

Sweet home Texas Riviera.

Leanna whammed on the screen door with a fist bathed in impatience. There was more fabric on the cannibalized recliner on the porch of said trailer than on Leanna's angry, angular frame. After a moment, a muscular young man in his mid-twenties wearing a sleeveless t-shirt and a blank expression appeared at the door. Michael Rundgren. Mikey to you. His soft, harmless face and spiky hairdo agreed with his tanned, toned, beefy body about as much as a French gymnast would with a Golden Corral.

Mikey grabbed a hold of Leanna, arm around her waist. It fit perfectly there.

"Shoot, Lee. Didn't know you was out. I thought you said—"

"I lied. Didn't want no one seeing me in there." Her body language growing more restless by the second, she looked around to see if any of the local hick busybodies were watching them from their double-wides."

"Aw babe, you didn't need to—" Mikey started as he went in for a kiss.

"You gonna let me in or what?" Leanna rebuffed his lips, more important business on her poison-tipped claymore of a brain. Both the explosive mine and the broadsword.

"Oh, right." Mikey finally opened up and Leanna blustered in. A puzzled look marched across Mikey's face as if it was returning from holiday in the Bahamas.

"You crashin' here?"

"Well, I don't got no other choice, do I?"

"Your mom still in Jamaica?"

"Haiti. Far as I know."

It was all she could do to keep from smacking Mikey right across his buttery, baby-assed cheek for mentioning the bitch, but the rare creature known only as Restraint reared its unicorn head and instead she pulled out one of the stolen purple pouches from her bag and dangled it in Mikey's face. Up close it looked like a worn-out Crown Royal sack tied up with craft store yarn.

Mikey's eyes locked in on the sack and almost dropped out of his head. But his deceptively muscley face kept them in check.

"That what I think it is?"

"Sure as shit, baby."

Mikey took it from Leanna and stared at it like it was the Holy Grail of something rednecks really get a kick out of. Maybe a combination of duck hunting and Mountain Dew Code Red.

He clapped his hands and rubbed them together with excited aggression. "We gonna do this?"

Leanna grinned a demon's grin and slipped off her top. Mikey moved to snap off her bra, but Leanna remembered what happened the last time he tried that and headed him off at the pass. "I got it," Leanna tried to say seductively, but it came out more like a wince. As they enjoined their mouths in a kiss that usually signified long-term involuntary celibacy, Leanna knew Teena hadn't corrupted him as she had so feared.

He's all mine. She'll never get her hands on him.
Ever.

~666~

Mikey's tin-can-on-wheels of a dwelling was a natural sweat magnet once inside. The fact that Leanna and Mikey were completely naked in bed, in the midst of hot and heavy foreplay, made such a sweat factor that much more prevalent. Taking a break from sucking on Mikey's tongue and humping his leg, Leanna poured some of the purple dust onto a mirror and chopped it up with a razor blade like it was some kind of freeze-dried unicorn-fart cocaine. It was time to activate the motherfucker of all catalysts.

Mikey smiled wide. He knew exactly what was about to transpire. They both took turns sniffing the dust greedily and proceeded to have the greatest one-on-one sex of all time. The dust switched their brains over to a slow-motion filter as they twisted and writhed around each other. Finding that perfect fit in the midst of pawing and scraping at skin, licking and sucking any significant bodily landmark. Mikey was rock hard against Leanna's drenched skin. She felt him rub his fleshy nightstick on her inner thighs and then soon after the outer walls of her labia. He was about to come on inside and wipe his feet on the welcome mat. She was ready for company. For a visitor. A tall, tanned, and muscular visitor with a perfectly proportioned cock.

"Now... Now, baby. No more teasing," Leanna's voice was unusually soft as she anticipated what was about to occur.

"Yes ma'am," Mikey whispered in her ear before sucking on her lobe. It drove Leanna to a place she hadn't been since before being locked up. She shuddered a little and grabbed his hands to help, unable to just wait patiently anymore. And with that, Mikey slid his cock inside of Leanna's slip-n-slide pussy and they both moaned in unison, filling his trailer with the synchronized sounds of unbridled pleasure. They were now two halves of a machine, working together to achieve maximum efficiency in the orgasm department.

Once Mikey was fully inside Leanna and had stroked her thoroughly for a solid three minutes or so, a litany of curse words filled the trailer as they both came to grips with their current reality. And that was the very precipice itself of mind-blowing orgasms for both of them. *Multiple* mind-blowing orgasms.

Pushing through a ripple of smaller orgasms that made her feel like she was on the sexiest banana boat being dragged around a pristine lake by the hottest motorboat captain in the harbor, Leanna felt herself getting close to the big one. She pushed on Mikey and gripped him hard, nails digging into his lower back as she wrapped her legs around his waist like a python to ensure he stayed the course. She was skirting the cliff, trying to edge her full orgasm as best as she could. But it had been a long time in prison, and she refused to fuck most of the bi skanks that wagged their tongues at her in there. This was the first true release for her in years. It was like a load of intoxicating nitroglycerine and the rickety truck carrying it was about to totter off the cliff and explode into smithereens.

"I'm gonna cum!" Leanna bellowed, lurching toward release. Her voice more like a drill sergeant than a lover.

Mikey was flummoxed. "I thought you just did."

"I'm gonna cum again, motherfucker!" She grabbed a clump of his hair and yanked, almost removing it from his scalp.

That sent Mikey over the edge as well. "Oh yeah, me too!"

"Really?" Leanna was impressed; this was a record for him. She had already felt him dump in her a few times and there were no weak spurts. This must be the big mama coming now. She braced herself as Mikey grunted a gargantuan orgasm in sync with Leanna's climaxing screams, like a pair of horny walruses trying to sing and run at the same time. He had to be spent by now. She felt like the milkman had tripped on his way up the steps and broke all his moo juice bottles right into her catcher's mitt. *No vacancy. All full up.*

They fell into a heap on the bed, naked and sweaty as all get out.

Mikey could barely express his thoughts into words. Even more than usual, that is.

"Ho-lee hell. That was—"

"I know." Leanna was already on his wavelength.

Mikey put his arms around Leanna to cuddle, but she rebuffed him, batting his trembling arms away.

"I didn't come here just to fuck."

"You didn't? Well there really is a first time for everything, ain't there?"

"I got a plan. And you're part of it."

"Does it involve *my* plan at all?"

Mikey's "plan" was to strike it rich making indie genre films with full-on porno sex scenes. He called them Reverse Bollywoods. She had to look up what that even meant. Several times. He'd been bugging her about it for years. Ever since they had sex for the first time in Teena's bedroom. Who knew her mom's sheets' thread count was muse?

"No. Fuck no. We're gonna find a way to sell this shit and make it big."

"Are you serious? Your mom—"

"Shut up with that shit. Fuck her."

"She's gonna mess you up fancy when she finds out you swiped her screw powder."

"She ain't gonna find out. And you didn't seem so against it earlier."

"Who's gonna turn down a roll with you, Lee? And what do you mean she ain't gonna find out, of course she—"

"I mean I got a plan to take care of her, too. And we ain't gonna be here when she gets back. I had a lot of time to think about this, okay?"

"Right. Well then, let's get going."

Mikey got up to get dressed, fumbling for everything all at once.

"Hold on, ya swingin' dick. Not yet."

"But she's gonna be back soon and—"

"We got some time. Gonna see Jiman about a buyer."

"Hell, that Rasta hobo ain't got no connections. Else he wouldn't be in this one horse of a town."

"Just let me do the thinking, babe."

The wheels started turning in Mikey's head. It was about goddamn time.

"How many guns you wanna bring?"

Now he was talking. Leanna let a killer's grin escape her face.

"How many you got?"

NINE...

Teena packed up her things in a small suitcase, humming something catchy yet foreboding to herself. Sounded like a satanic rendition of "Sweet Chariot."

The energy expended during her couché ceremony seemed like it would never return. As if it were out there in the ether, loathe to return to her unspectacular existence.

What she saw in her mind's eye in the blackness still frightened her. It was all she could do to keep from randomly screaming out loud whenever someone asked her if she was okay. Many people asked if she was okay. Repeatedly. Without any concern for whether or not she was *actually* okay. Like someone had put them up to just mindlessly asking her.

Before she could finish packing her meager belongings, Mama Francine strolled in with a disappointed look on her face. It felt fake, though. Lately a lot of things about her felt fake. It didn't alarm Teena. In fact, it felt just a little bit normal.

Mama Francine placed a hand on Teena's rigid shoulder. She stopped folding clothes and just stood there, waiting for whatever Mama Francine was going to inevitably say.

"I was hoping you would stay with us at least a little longer, dearie."

Teena responded inside her head, then realized she need to actually say it out loud if she wanted her to go away eventually. Sooner rather than later.

"I know. I wanted to. I want to. It's just—"

"Leanna." Mama Francine spat out her name like it was a disease.

"She's getting out of the halfway home next month and I wanted to—I need to prepare for her release. Regardless of what happens between us."

Mama Francine crossed her arms as Teena dropped a half-folded blouse, head down.

"I just think she needs someone stable to guide her now more than ever."

"If what you told me is true, Teena, that girl is more trouble than she is worth. You gave her more chances than anyone else would ever give her."

Mama Francine's tone had changed from parental to chiding on a dime. A flattened, dull dime. Teena just wanted to be alone more than anything else. Even though that's when the blackness returned to taunt her. It was preferable now to Mama Francine's off-putting aura. She could sense it plain as day ever since she awoke from the ceremony.

"I'm...her mother. I can't just put a limit on her chances. It's my fault she's—"

Even Teena didn't believe her own words as they came out. It just felt like something a mother should say, in case anyone was listening.

And who would that be? That shadow-soaked thing behind you, just out of sight?

44

"That girl is going to be the death of you if you aren't careful, dearie."

Teena embraced Mama Francine tightly. Her very own attempt at fake concern toward someone else.

"I'll be back. As soon as I sort things out with her, I'll come back."

There's no way in hell I'm coming back. Hector knows. He knows what's out there.

"I know. I just worry about you, child. You were my first. *Are* my first."

A slip of the tongue? Mama Francine's reach is far. But to Corpus Christi? A long, useless reach indeed.

"I'll be okay, Mama. I need to do this."

Mama Francine lightened her tone with a forced smile. Teena sensed the woman no longer wished to be in the same room with her. Instead of feeling enlightened, it just made her more unhappy inside her own body.

"If you think of it, be sure to stop in and see Della Suzanne. She mentioned you last time I spoke with her."

She did?

Teena's face involuntarily lit up a little. There was no hiding her feelings for Della Suzanne. Even after what she just went through.

"Don't disappoint her now."

It meant a trip to Austin, of all places. But if Della had indeed asked about Teena, she would find the time to go.

Maybe Leanna would come with me. It would be good for us.

Teena snorted at that last thought, wanting to smack herself for such blind naiveté. She knew what really had to be done. But could she do it? Could she actually—

"I will miss you greatly, my Tee-Tee."

Ugh. Teena gagged internally. The pet name approach. Mama Francine was pulling out all the stops tonight.

Mama Francine kissed her on the forehead and made for the door with a curt smile. Before she was gone, she stopped for a second and turned back to Teena with an odd look. A look that was hollow and concerned all at once. Her aura changed. From indifferent to slightly fearful.

"As I said earlier, you will see things, dearie. Maybe you already are. Maybe not. But you will see things. Your instinct will be to convince yourself that they are all in your mind. I assure you they are not. For some, the veil is lifted a little bit. Something seen out of the corner of your eye, a whisper from nearby when you're alone in the night. But for those whom the veil is lifted all the way; they might as well be living in another world entirely. I just want you to know I've been there. And I know you will do what must be done in the long run."

Teena nodded slightly; her brain fixed on what her mentor had just said. No words came, though. Not enough energy to comprehend and speak at the same time now.

With that, Mama Francine finished her exit completely. Teena would have bet money that she heard Mama say something low and slow once she was outside. Something Teena desperately didn't want to hear. Something about not being able to see Teena's aura, maybe?

The quiet that remained in the hut with Teena was deafening and more than a little alarming to her sensibilities. She could feel tiny hands gently touching her skin. Benign probing, prodding. Inquisitive. Alien.

To combat the feeling of desperate loneliness, Teena returned to that sweet, intoxicating humming as she finished packing. A hymn designed to stave off the darkness and simultaneously put her enemies at ease.

<u>TEN...</u>

The Cluck Shack.

The seediest of seedy diners, specializing in chicken and waffles. And meth. The hideous layout is all 1970s yellows and oranges. Romper Room for hobos and pimps. It was cruel irony in a way that the food was actually really fucking good. You just had to be copasetic with the high chance of being mugged in your quest for the tastiest tenders this side of the Mississippi.

Leanna and Mikey were crammed into a booth, coffee in hand. As Leanna scanned the worn interior décor, she smiled at the memory of giving Joey Garvin a handjob in the ladies' bathroom. It made Mikey jealous enough to break Joey's arm and get back together with her for the third time.

"What are ya thinkin' about?" Mikey asked, more than a little defensive.

Leanna chuckled without ever making eye contact with Mikey. "Just remembering the good times. Happy to be out is all."

"I bet. Why don't we just go back to my place and forget this whole Jiman jazz, huh babe?"

Leanna barely even registered his semi-desperate request. Her eyes were doing their own feverish search for Jiman.

"He'll be here. Don't worry."

"Huh? That ain't what I asked, Lee. You on this planet right now?"

After a moment, a tall and skinny young man with a huge Jamaican Rasta beanie and dirty clothes shuffled over to their booth. Leanna showed him all her teeth with an eager smile and waved him over even though he was nearly there already. Jiman never liked Mikey and his disgust showed through as he harrumphed while he sat down.

"You smell like a nursing home." Mikey's attempt at rapier wit made Leanna grunt in embarrassment.

Jiman just went for the direct approach. "You smell like a fucking idiot."

"Whatever," Mikey murmured, bringing his coffee mug to his lips and averting his eyes.

"Good to see you out, convict. That parking attendant you violated is suing the city. You dodged a bullet on that one," Jiman gloated as he bobbed his lazy head with every syllable that came out of his mouth, as if he were emphasizing a point only he could comprehend.

"I have my ways," Leanna said, unimpressed with Jiman's news update.

"Like what? Did you fuck a city council member?"

"I fucked all of them."

"Jesus Christ, Leanna, I was just joking."

"That's cute."

"Ain't she great?" Mikey tried to wedge his way into a conversation he was clearly not invited to. Jiman sized up Mikey and *hmphed* through his closed mouth. "So what do you two upstanding citizens want?"

"Got something to sell." Leanna was eager to get to the point and almost spilled it all right there. *Patience, baby. Patience.*

"Usually, that's my job."

"We're thinking bigger than you on this one. No offense."

"The fuck you need me for then?"

"Your connections. This is big. Real big."

"I told you, he ain't got no connections 'sides the same Rasta bums he bangs around with." There was Mikey again, knocking on the door to Club Conversation. Just begging to be let in.

"Shut the fuck up, Mike. People with brains is talking." Jiman rarely ever sounded threatening, but when it came to Mikey, everything out of his mouth was hostile.

Leanna pulled out the purple pouch and slid it to Jiman. "Snort this shit with whoever you like fucking the best. Your head will explode after about the seventh consecutive orgasm. Makes Miss Molly feel like a bad case of the shingles."

Jiman sized up the pouch. Opened it up. Sniffed the stuff. He even tried to taste some before Leanna grabbed his hand more than a little forcefully.

"Hey, what'd I say? Wait 'til you're ready to screw. You do it in here and you'll jerk yourself off all over the god damn lunch counter."

"You fucking with me? Cuz if you are—"

"Just try it."

Jiman squinted at them in utter disbelief.

Leanna leaned in towards him and continued her salacious pitch. "That should be enough for you and a buddy, whoever that is. When you're all done, call me and we'll talk. Got it?"

"Okay, okay. Jesus. But if you're fucking with me, I ain't selling you no more of nothing, my lady. Dig?"

Leanna smiled. The cat was in the bag and on the way to Cat in the Bag City, USA.

"I dig."

ELEVEN...

"*Delta Flight 1232 to St. Paul now departing from Gate A14. Final call for Delta Flight 1232 to St. Paul. Departs from Gate A14.*"

Teena sat in a seemingly forgotten terminal at DFW International Airport on her layover. Eyes closed, humming quietly. She was fondling that same lock of blonde hair again. The only part of Leanna she could control. At least that's what she told herself when it was quiet.

Flight departure announcements buzzed intermittently. The area was sparsely filled, only a dozen or so other people waited for their flights. Most likely returning to families eagerly awaiting their arrival.

Must be nice.

A creaky creak of a man in his late sixties walked past Teena, then backed up, sniffed, and approached her. He wore a loud Hawaiian shirt his wife probably hated. His off-brand sneakers squeaked on the floor as he stopped directly in front of her.

"Excuse me..."

Teena stifled a sigh. She was proud of her restraint this soon back in the States.

Ah, yes. Back to the real world. The world of men. And their insistences.

"...Pardon me, miss."

Teena opened her eyes and met the man's unblinking gaze.

He had a goofy smile that spoke of a suburban life of unchallenged ease. It reminded her of her old neighbors. Useless and intrusive.

"Yes?"

"I hate to impose, but would you mind terribly telling me what kind of perfume you're wearing? It's absolutely intoxicating, and I just know my wife would die for some."

Teena quelled another laugh and smiled sweetly at him. *Of course.* She had forgotten about her perfume. Beetle pheromones and fermented vanilla. Plus a few other secret ingredients. Spanish Fly for weak-minded men. That meant most of them.

"Oh, why thank you. But you can't get it anywhere around here, I'm afraid. It's imported, my love."

He seemed downright hypnotized by her smell as well as her presence.

Damn. I must have put too much on. This will make the cab ride home a chore.

"Oh. Where can I get it?"

In Hell. Care to go?

"Anything else I can do for you, my dear?"

He swayed back and forth, nigh intoxicated.

"Oh, no. That's okay. Thank you. My apologies for bothering you."

"Anytime, sweetie. Be good and love always."

She was barely able to get those words out without choking on them. She used to believe them. Then she awoke from that darkness. It was all she could do to keep from lobbing obscenities at passersby now.

He left with a drunken smile on his lips. She went back to humming and playing with that lock of hair. Intermittently looking for stray shadows standing behind pillars or sitting in a distant seat just out of the corner of her eye.

The closer she got to home, the more she thought about the avalanche of pride she was going to have to swallow to make it work with her daughter, the more she wanted to call it all off. As she was leaving Mama's village in Haiti, it started like a benign growth. By the time she was stewing in DFW, it was a full-blown malignant carcinoma. Impeding on her brain. Clouding her vision.

Ruining my blessed day.

Was that a shadow over there? Behind the empty departure desk at gate A17?

Teena's eyes darted all around the terminal. This was supposed to be a safe place. An antiseptic place. No death here.

Or was there?

It was foolish to think anything other than death being everywhere at all times.

"I have a lot of cleaning to do. She'll be home before you know it," Teena said out loud in a forcefully cheerful voice to absolutely no one at all.

TWELVE...

The first time Leanna heard of the dust was after one of Teena's late-night dates with her newest man about town. Her mother was drunk and fixing for an argument with Leanna. Pointing out her faults as a teenager to deflect against her own faults as an adult. Shitty Parenting 101.

It was in the middle of said argument, during a show-stopping tirade, Teena let slip its very existence. She had kept it so secret from Leanna for so long. But Teena was lonely, and Leanna knew she felt helpless and trapped with her in that house on the edge of the city. Finally bragging about her creation was inevitable, drunk or not. In between exaltations and condemnations of her husband, Leanna's father, Teena sneered at Leanna about the one thing she had over her. A drug that could make any man (or woman for that matter) love her unconditionally. Leanna remembered distinctly the drop of her own jaw at this revelation. It had to be bullshit. But then Teena brought it out from the hope chest where she kept it locked away. Fine-grained purple sand that smelled like lilacs and dried blood. Leanna never forgot that smell. It haunted her from then on. As Teena locked it away again, Leanna asked if she could use it one day and Teena just laughed at her before informing her daughter that no one would ever want to love her, even under the effects of a love potion. That one hurt. That night was the first time Leanna legitimately cried herself to sleep. Looking back, the sheer essence of that night itself has kept her going all this time. Her hatred of Teena dined off that memory for years and it still did.

~666~

As Leanna and Mikey fucked again, this time doggystyle, Leanna mused on the fact that Teena's boast of unconditional love at the hands of the dust wasn't exactly how it really worked. More like unconditional lust. *Temporary* unconditional lust.

Leanna hung off the side of the bed, head halfway to the floor. Mikey dripped a reservoir of sweat as he tried to literally nail her directly into said floor. The dust was pumping like a freight train through their veins. Their sex was wild, aggressive, and louder than a shootout in a whorehouse. Unhindered by any thought or threat of returning to normalcy afterwards.

They had sniffed so much in such a short time, there was a literal purple haze enveloping the entire trailer. It made Leanna's eyes dry and bleary. Mikey coughed in between bullish grunts.

Leanna's phone rang, interrupting their rhythm.

"Don't answer it, babe. I'm working on my sixth nut," Mikey whined through his grunting.

Leanna pie-faced him in impressive fashion from where she was located. "It's Jiman. Get. Off."

Mikey ceased drilling and Leanna broke the seal, scrambling for the phone.

"Aw, Lee. Hurry up before I find something else to poke. I can't stop this train."

Leanna pictured Mikey frantically fucking the old hole she made with one of her chunky heels years ago in his bedroom wall and it almost made her laugh. Almost. One of them had to be the adult.

"Shut up," she said as she answered the phone, breathy and still in the throes of pleasure. "Yeah?"

She could hear the sounds of hot, hard, and loud sex over the phone. At least two or three people were getting their love dust groove on.

"...Meet...me at the Cluck Shack...tomorrow...noon." Jiman's voice sounded relieved and sickly all at once. And then someone on his end of the phone orgasmed harder than an Italian nun using a dildo molded from Christ's cock.

"Ha! You like that shit!?" Leanna was so pleased with herself she reached for Mikey's dick to tug on in celebration. He backed away with a frown, shaking his head "no" adamantly.

"And bring more!"

Someone else orgasmed hard over the phone. It sounded like they were screaming for their mother. Leanna couldn't relate. Jiman hung up in the middle of it all without another word.

Leanna felt like her head was about to gently float off her neck with a rubbery squeak and take her brain straight to heaven. This was it. Her horny ship of money had finally come in. And it was all at her mother's expense. All she could muster from her upturned mouth was "Holy shit".

"So?" Mikey asked as if he wasn't even in the room for what just happened. Batting his dick between his clammy hands, still harder than differential calculus.

"It's on, bitch! It's motherfucking on!"

Leanna hugged Mikey in the pure joy of celebration while he just hooted and hollered and aggressively humped Leanna's leg with his unabated rod.

She was fine with it. Things were about to change for the good around here and a little spunk on her leg was a whole heap of nothing now.

Hump away, Mikey. Hump away.

THIRTEEN...

Pulling up to her own house after so long away and in such a shabby cab made Teena feel she was returning to prison from an extended work release program. No one around to appreciate her passions. No one to care about her dreams. Just a steady diet of good old fashioned American indifference. The house was pitch black save for a light on inside at the far end of the façade. She smirked a bit when she spotted it.

Ronnie must still be here. But why was he in Teena's room?

As she got out of the back of the cab, an Ernest Borgnine stunt double of a cabbie popped the trunk and rushed to grab her bags. Teena took them from him and handed over a wad of cash. He smiled the same drunken smile as the old guy from the airport.

"Are you sure you can't get it around here? I'll pay whatever it—"

"Trust me, my love. If I could give it to you for free, I would. That's a promise."

"Aw... Okay, then."

"Thank you, my darling. Stay safe and be sweet."

The Cabbie staggered back into his taxi and drove off as Teena headed to the front door. Reaching for her keys, she saw the door ajar.

Maybe it wasn't Ronnie.

Mikey? No. He wouldn't dare.

Teena flipped a light switch in the hall and looked around, ready for anything.

"Ronnie...?"

Nothing.

"Michael T. Rundgren, if you're in here, I swear on the Maiden..."

Her tone was sufficiently menacing yet it yielded nothing different. The house remained a void.

She headed down the hall. The closed door at the far end had the light coming through it.

Her eyes locked on each empty room she passed as she advanced down the hallway. Dark. Empty. No ambush. Yet.

As she reached the end of the hall, she knocked gently on the old door belonging to Leanna's old room.

"Ronnie, baby? You sleeping?"

She opened the door...

~666~

I remember the good times. Our times. The times we could get away from her. That night you gave me that adorable little promise ring I knew her influence on you had ended. We could be together without her scorn. Her disapproving grunts and curses. It wasn't perfect. But when is true love ever perfect? People would ask if I was your mother. Embarrassing for some, sure. But it turned me on. And I know it turned you on as well. Like we were getting away with something forbidden. I knew in my heart I was saving you. Saving you from her and her abuses. Her expectations. We had to do something. Something had to be done. Right? To make sure she couldn't interfere.

60

To make sure she couldn't hurt you. I should have stayed. I should have never left. I could have protected you. She never would have done this if I were here. Remember that first time we went to the movies, and you let me pick the movie? It seems small. Insignificant. But living with her left little time to choose anything. Even something as forgettable as a Friday night movie. I knew before but it was a silly, stupid thought. Now I know for sure. I know what needs to be done. God damn it all, she's going to make me walk alone through the rest of this half-assed life.

~666~

Teena sat next to the corner cupboard in her front room, her voodoo room, eyes red and wet. She softly hummed to herself, arms around her legs, rocking back and forth. The broken urn and ash sat in a neat pile next to her.

The humming calmed her, helped her focus on what needed to be done next. She saw Ronnie's face again and moaned like a wounded animal through her humming.

After a long moment, she whipped her head towards the hope chest in the corner. The blanket was askew, and the lock was broken. She rushed over and flung the lid open, eyes darting wildly.

She wouldn't...

She went through everything in the trunk until she fully registered the unmistakable absence of the things that should never, ever be missing from their resting place.

"No, no, no, no... Don't do this to me... Please..."

They *had* to be there somewhere. She threw the contents around, increasingly frantic in her search. Her purple pouches.

Gone. She screamed in frustration, falling backwards onto the floor. After a futile bout of calming her breathing and attempting to hum again, she went into a fit of manic, uncontrollable laughter. The house itself seemed to flinch and shudder at such a frightening disturbance.

Of course she would.

~666~

Hours later, Teena rocked back and forth in an old rocking chair next to the hope chest, humming yet again. Centering herself in what now felt like a continuous cycle of uncontrollable outrage followed by fake calm.

It was all gone. All of it. Everything she had worked for. The dust. Ronnie. Her sanity. How could she be so stupid to think Leanna could change?

Tired of the mediation charade, she rose and headed back over to the hope chest, reached behind it, and unlocked a secret compartment in the back. She pulled out an old, musty book with an ominous title.

Caplatas & Evil Intent

Her conversation with Mama Francine echoed in her head...

"You haven't tried it on your own have you?"

"What? Why would you... I would never—"

"Good. You don't need to be messing with such things just yet. Trying to reconnect the spirit to the body after more than a few days is a recipe for misery. Trust me, I would know."

Teena embraced the book and held it near to her, caressing it tightly. Then, she looked back down the hallway toward the bedroom, wiping her tears away with a weird smile.

This has to be done.

FOURTEEN...

L eanna and Mikey barged into the Cluck Shack like a couple of senior citizens homing in on the slots at a shitty off-strip casino. Jiman was spread out in a booth, looking as if he'd just run a marathon. Sunglasses on, nursing coffee. They eventually found their way over to him, coming off just as tired.

Leanna almost guffawed at the sight of Jiman's empty husk.

"Long night?"

"I'd say the same about you," Jiman groaned.

"You bet your ass. Didn't even sleep a fucking wink. We got a deal?"

Jiman mustered all his remaining energy to take a few gulps of his coffee and take off his sunglasses. His eyes were bloodshot all to shit. It made both Mikey and Leanna mouth a hearty *"Wow"*.

"Gimme another one of them bags," Jiman croaked.

Leanna pulled out another purple pouch and tossed it to Jiman. He held on to it and caressed it like a long-lost love.

"It's a limited supply kind of thing. I ain't made of this stuff. Not yet at least."

"So I deduced legit you're looking for a buyer that can reverse engineer this shit and mass produce it. Yes, no?"

"Bingo, baby."

Jiman looked around, paranoid. Waited a moment for a waitress to pass by.

"I know a guy out west, yeah."

Leanna and Mikey lean in closer.

"Arizona. Just outside of Tucson—"

"Tucson, baby! Yeah." Mikey clapped his hands and clucked.

Jiman and Leanna gawked at him like he had a penis growing out of a penis growing out of his mouth.

"Can I fucking finish, retard? Can I? You cool with me finishing what you came to hear?" If Jiman had possessed the correct amount of energy to backhand Mikey, he absolutely would have done so.

"Sure, knock yourself out," Mikey whispered as he scratched his head, looking to see if the waitress saw him make a fool of himself. Par for the course.

Jiman continued, his voice painfully breaking down into a decayed groan. "Name's Drakesworth. Runs Molly and H out a warehouse on the outskirts. Number one supplier out there, I'm told. Get most of my shit from his guys roundabouts. If anyone can take care of you, it's him."

Leanna snorted. "Drakesworth? Is he a fucking butler?"

"Yeah you go ahead and tell that to his face and let me know how that works out for you. Besides, not a one knows his *real* name. And Lee, he ain't nobody to fuck with. This guy's the real deal Holyfield."

"I bet he is. So that's it, huh?" Leanna sounded unimpressed and Jiman's face grew more annoyed with every disrespect she communicated.

Mikey was ready to leave and demonstrated so by just getting the fuck up. "Nice knowing you, Jiman." Leanna surprisingly followed suit. Mikey puffed up just a bit at that.

"Wait a minute. You're on parole, sweet thing. And you're a walking accessory, bright boy. How you gonna get out of the state?"

"Don't you worry about it. That happens to be next on my latest to-do list. Just tell that Drakesworth fella we're on our way."

"Oh, he already knows you're coming. For real."

"Good. We'll make a grand fucking entrance, then."

"Words to the wise. Keep a low profile and don't do nothing fucked up on the way, in the way, around the way, no way."

"I'm reformed, Jimmy. Don't you worry about us. A little ol' cross country road trip will do us wonders, right baby?"

"You want me to boost my dad's Jag?" Mikey sounded prouder than an entire Pride parade as he presented that option.

Jiman was just gobsmacked. "What in the fuck did I just say about a low profile? Is he for real?"

"He is. And he's all I got," Leanna beamed and put an arm around Mikey's waist.

Mikey semi-blushed at that. "Thanks, baby. Love you too."

"Good luck and so on and so forth," Jiman managed to squeeze from his used-tube-of-toothpaste mouth.

Mikey and Leanna headed for the door. Leanna turned back to Jiman for a second, an important question nagging at her grey matter.

"How many people you fuck last night?"

"Eight," Jiman said without moving a muscle or even looking back at her.

"Fucking *eight*?"

"Yeah."

Leanna turned back and left the Cluck Shack to its own asinine devices with Mikey in tow.

Jiman soon passed out in the booth, a low-level drug king on his cracked pleather throne snoring the snore of a sexually over-satisfied lout.

FIFTEEN...

"She'll never stop hating me."

Deep in the woods, Teena stood in front of an unmarked grave with a large, weathered stone cross. It couldn't be a legal gravesite. It was so very far from anything else.

The sun had almost left the building completely and shadows threw their weight around with reckless abandon.

Teena looked as if she'd been crying just minutes before, her eyes puffy and red. She leaned on an old, long, and gnarled walking staff.

She was proud of her handiwork when it came to this specific burial site. She wished she had visited more often in recent years, but the inescapable quicksand of life with Leanna pretty much forbade it. Her daughter couldn't know of this place. *Shouldn't* know of it. Ever.

The quiet all around her would wig out a librarian. No birds or anything.

"I should never have come back. I could have stayed over there. Belonged to something. Here I'm just another nobody. That's exactly what she thinks of me."

Every time she finished speaking, she leaned in as if to listen to the headstone talk. Reply.

"What? No. At the end of the day I can't just abandon her. Our fates are tied together. Even if she's bent on dragging me down, I won't give her the satisfaction."

Another creeping pause. She laughed. It invaded the quiet. Unwelcome. The shadows themselves seemed to flinch at the sound.

"Oh no, but it is nice to see you again. Even if nothing good comes of finding her, I'll still have you in my life."

She looked behind her as if she knew someone was watching her. The blackness felt near. They were peering at her through the shadows. Laughing at her stupidity. Her loneliness. She returned her gaze to the grave, sighing the sigh of a tired woman beyond mundane reasoning.

"I hate to ask a favor of you, darling. But I'm going to need you to do something especially important for me."

She waited politely for a response.

"Splendid. I am in your debt, my love."

SIXTEEN...

A nasty, skeevy row of white trash establishments. You'd think it was anywhere in Florida if not for the existence of Texas. Leanna was dressed in a tight purple pleather miniskirt and tiger-striped tube top with see-through stripper heels, clutching a bottle of medium-priced champagne wrapped in a bow. She pounded on the glass front door to Killford's office until she saw an intercom. She pressed the button hastily and several times.

"Ain't Friday yet, Forsythe. Phone call would suffice until then."

"It's important. I needed to see you."

She grinned super fake and super wide, hoping it would translate through the security camera.

"Real bad."

Buzzzzzz.

~666~

Killford's office was covered in paperwork, food wrappers, and beer cans. And her clothes. All of them. And all of Leanna's clothes. Killford was straddled in her office chair, legs up like she was giving birth. Leanna was down at the business end of her parole officer, giving her the best tongue job of her life.

"Oh god! I'm gonna...I'm gonna..!"

Killford convulsed, bucked her hips something fierce, and went limp. As she huffed and puffed, her hand searched for a pack of cigarettes on her desk. Then, a lighter.

Leanna got up and wiped her mouth with a shaky hand. Hiding her disgusted frown, she rubbed her raw knees. They were screaming balls of red-hot fire poker pain at that point. She'd been down there for hours and felt like she was in a fugue state. Killford's eyes found hers and she gave Leanna a weak thumbs up.

"I haven't... It's been... Oh hell, that was just nice," Killford murmured with a cig hanging out of her mouth.

"Which one?"

"All seven of 'em. You okay?"

"Yeah. Fine," Leanna sighed as she shook out her legs and continued to rub her knees.

The bulls in prison never had me down there that long. Fuckaroni rigatoni with this bitch.

"Want me to return the favor?" Killford nodded at Leanna's crotch.

"Actually, I do."

Killford hopped out of her chair and dropped to her knees right in front of Leanna, cigarette still in her mouth.

"Wait, that's not what I had in mind."

"Anal? I got a couple nice-sized—"

"No! I mean, normally that would sound right up my alley. But—"

"Shit. You mean a real favor. The trouble kind."

"Only if no one knows."

"Forsythe—"

"I just need to leave the state. Temporarily. Arizona temporarily. I'll be back in a week. I promise."

Killford got up and started to dress, cigarette still hanging in there.

"I suppose you ain't gonna tell me what for."

"Plausible deniability?"

"You must think I'm some real stupid Sally you can just munch on and get your way with, huh?"

"I thought it was a good plan..."

Killford took a swig of the champagne Leanna brought. Cigarette still hanging from her clammy lips. Leanna was impressed.

"At the time."

"You're gonna sell that dust, I wager."

"It's big money. We'll cut you in. Plus more dust. And more me if you want. I promise. If we don't come back you can come after us, lock us up and throw away the key."

"We? You leaving with that Rundgren kid? That ain't a good idea."

"He's harmless. Unless I tell him what to do."

"I don't take well to threats."

"Just being honest."

Killford put out her cigarette in the champagne bottle and lit another one. She was half-dressed at that point and still shaking from the Seven Orgasms of Leanna Forsythe.

"You got one week. If you ain't back by sunup next Wednesday, you're looking at the rest of your life behind bars."

Leanna grabbed a hold of Killford and kissed her sincere thanks right onto her smoky champagne lips.

"Thanks. You won't regret it," Leanna cooed.

"Me not regretting anything is the only way you stay a free little bird."

Leanna dressed quickly and tossed Killford the rest of a purple pouch.

"You can have this one. Compliments of the house."

"You sure this stuff is safe?"

"You ask me that after you've had some?"

"Now I'm thinking clear."

"It's perfectly safe. Unless you're fucking in open traffic or something."

"Just get out of here."

"You're the best."

Leanna kissed her on the cheek and left in a flash.

Killford finished dressing and took a long drag off her cigarette.

"Hmph. Women."

SEVENTEEN...

Teena leaned on her walking staff, staring at a massive, dead tree in front of her. She was even deeper into the woods. No one had been there, not even hunters, in years. She had put a curse on this place. Where the gravesite from earlier was quiet, almost serene, this site screamed of the dead and decay. It was extremely dark in every way imaginable. She had just an electric lantern hanging from a branch for light.

Through the void, Teena stared obsessively at something scratched on the necrotic bark.

"It's official now," she murmured, in a deep trance.

~666~

I remember that night so well. Like a scene from a classic film. You took me for a walk. You always loved walks. I loved that you loved the simple things in life. It was never complicated with you. A walk and a talk. A hug and a smile. It meant the world to me. And I know it meant the same to you. You took me to our tree. The one we said was our secret castle. Our hideaway. Whenever things got rough, we went there to get away. From the world. From everyday life. From her. I knew she would try to take you. To spoil you. Spoil your pristine soul. She would try. But I knew you wouldn't let her. You were too good for her. And me. You brought me to our tree that day and showed me what you had done. Our initials carved in our tree. T + W. Forever. You were thinking of forever. I'm ashamed to admit I could only think of the next time. The next time I could have a quiet moment away from her. Now I wish I had been dreaming of something much larger. Something much longer. You had me beat in that department. You knew. We could have done it. Together. Forever. We can still do it. We can still make her pay.

~666~

Teena was still staring at the same tree. "T+W Forever" etched into the bark.

"It's still our spot. She can't take that away from us."

Teena pulled out her *Caplatas & Evil Intent* book and thumbed through the pages until she found what she was looking for.

With a grim face, she stared at the tree's engraving again. After a moment, Teena chanted in broken French from the book, her voice got lower and deeper with each phrase. Her hand shook, ruffling the book. Her words echoed ominously all around her.

The ground in front of the tree rumbled and shook. Crunching and cracking sounds rose from the dirt. A hand broke free. Another hand followed quickly. Both rotting and putrid. A head poked through. The head of a dead, decaying man with short hair and a patchwork beard. Poor Wallis. Teena wasn't terrified or disgusted by this at all. In fact, she was smiling.

After a few more moments, Wallis was completely up and out from his dirt birth. He stood awkwardly, swaying his head but never moving his eyes from Teena. She reached back into her shoulder bag and pulled out some horn-rimmed glasses.

"Almost forgot," she smiled as she held them up to his face.

He just stared at the glasses for a moment, as if he didn't even understand what they were.

"Go on, silly. They're all yours."

Wallis reached with a creaky jerk and grabbed them loosely. He fidgeted with them for a moment before putting them on, poking himself in the eye several times before succeeding.

"Wallis, my love. There you are."

Wallis vomited up a nasty black goo and promptly ate some. Then, he looked back up at Teena with a puppy dog smile and heavy panting.

"Leeeannnnaaaaa...."

His voice was an untuned piano going from high notes to much lower, darker notes as he droned on.

Teena inhaled deep and nodded. "I know, baby. I know."

EIGHTEEN...

The Cluck Shack looked kind of regal at night. If your idea of regal was an unwanted reach-around from a leper with a passion for showtunes.

Leanna and Mikey leaned on Mikey's car, a grey '91 Pontiac Trans Am in surprisingly good condition. They shared a joint, waiting for someone's arrival that Leanna both anticipated and dreaded.

"I wonder how many drug deals go down here. I mean like real stats and what not."

Mikey was in full-on ponder mode and Leanna refused to answer.

"What about contracts? I wonder how many contracts on people's lives get okayed out here."

"Hold on, let me go buy a megaphone so you can broadcast it to the whole fucking world."

"I can't believe you balled that lesbo, Lee. I mean, what the hell?"

"Already explained to you why. And you ain't never been mad before when I fucked somebody else."

"Well now I'm starting to. She wasn't even that hot."

"Christ, is that all you think about? Hot or not? We ain't got no chance in hell of making that payday if we got her after us."

"I know, I know. But still."

"I said you could fuck Sue-Ellen Mackey at that Mardi Gras party. She was tellin' everyone who would listen what she was gonna do to you."

"Sue-Ellen Mackey's got herpes."

"Don't we all?"

"No. Wait, do *you*?"

"That's not the point. You had your chance and you turned it down. I ain't responsible for what's going on in some other skank's plumbing."

"Wait a minute, Lee—"

Right then, a piss-faded yellow, mid-1980s Buick LeSabre with a busted driver's side headlight pulled up two spaces away from them.

"*This* is the guy?" Mikey asked, clearly unimpressed.

A scraggly, gangly man in acid-wash jeans and a faded bomber jacket got out and strolled into the Cluck Shack without even looking at them. His outfit was completed by aviator sunglasses and alligator boots.

Ricky Richards in the goddamned flesh. I got scum-chills all up and down my back on account of the sight of such a man.

"I bet you a whole sack of fuck dust it is," Leanna whisper-smiled.

Mikey cocked his head like an old dog. "I'll take that bet. Wait, I mean—"

Leanna grabbed him by the arm and made for the entrance.

~666~

Ricky Richards sat in a booth by himself at the back of the diner. Leanna and Mikey were at the door, frozen. The place was empty

78

besides them, except for a cute waitress in her twenties and the old, chubby cook who looked at least twenty years past retirement.

"Do we sit with him?" Mikey wondered.

Leanna squeezed his arm as if she'd just remembered something from another life. "I've seen this before in a shitty movie. You're supposed to sit in a different booth, like one next to him and we talk like that."

"Oh, good idea."

They tiptoed to the booth behind Richards and slid in. The waitress scooted over to bring Richards his coffee.

"Thanks, sugar."

"Aw, it ain't nothin'."

"I mean I want sugar. Now."

The waitress left, the picture of embarrassment.

"Don't ask us for nothin' or whatever!" Mikey yelled at the fleeing waitress.

"Shut the fuck up," Leanna fumed.

The waitress brought Richards some sugar and slid over to Mikey and Leanna's table, pen and pad ready.

"What can I get you two?"

"Just a coffee. Black. No sugar, sugar," Leanna said with a quiver of a laugh in her voice.

The waitress faked a smile. Mikey rubbed his hands together in delicious anticipation. "I'll have the Cluck-a-Buck platter and an extra order of fries—"

Leanna kicked Mikey under the table.

"Sweet tea is all. Thanks," he mumbled, more than a little crestfallen.

The waitress left without a word and the diner grew silent as hell.

"You two green-horned chicken hoppers gonna come sit over here or are we gonna play telephone footsie all night?"

Mikey elbowed Leanna, who elbowed him even harder. They got up and scooched into the booth containing Richards, sitting opposite him. Mikey extended his hand to him.

"How's it goin', boss?"

Richards just stared at the hand, then looked at Leanna. She just merely like it happened all the time.

"You got my money, junebug?"

Leanna nudged Mikey. He dropped his hand and pulled out a wrinkled brown paper bag from his shorts.

"How much?" Ricky asked as he eyeballed the bag.

"Five grand," Leanna said, pleased with herself.

"That's only half. Hit the bricks." Richards sipped his coffee dismissively and stared at the waitress's ass. She returned soon after with Mikey and Leanna's drinks.

"You make some new friends over here?" The waitress said with a slight chuckle, trying to ease the tension.

"I'll make friends with *you* if you don't mind your fucking business," Ricky said through his tilted coffee mug.

The poor waitress skulked off to a far corner of the diner.

"It's all I got. C'mon, man. We're good for it," Mikey reasoned, reaching out a fist in hopes of a return bump from Richards. When in doubt, Mikey bumped. It was his last resort to diffuse a sticky situation. Leanna hated and admired it in equal measures.

"You're good for it? What I see is a bricks-for-brains musclehead with a whistling breeze blowin' through his fuckin' ears and a convicted felon on parole with a bad attitude and a great set of tits. Good for it don't come near the fact of the matter."

Leanna had remained polite for long enough. It was time to set the record straight with this rat-faced hayseed. "Look, you shit-kickin' Richard Petty lookin' motherfucker, we're giving you five grand now and a hell of a lot more than that when we get back. All I fucking asked is for you take care of that bitch while we're gone, and this is yours right now. Don't act like you don't need it, shitwad."

Richards stewed, clenching his fists. "You don't know nothin' 'bout me, spitfire."

"I know your wife left you cuz you got one of them transgendered porn stars on the side that you let fuck you in the ass as long as she wears Mrs. Richards' clothes."

Mikey snorted a gulp of sweet tea right out of his nose. Both nostrils.

"That ain't true," Richards gritted through his teeth.

"Sharnell Corrino. I *know* that bitch. You ain't the only one who can find shit out, Dick."

Richards took another measured sip of his coffee and snatched the money from Mikey.

"How much more on the back end?"

"A fucking lot." Leanna smacked the table in excitement as she answered him.

Mikey felt like he had to "help" and added "Yeah, once we sell—"

Leanna kicked Mikey right in the balls, causing him to change course immediately.

"Uh... Once we sell my dad's sports car. We should clean up something fierce. He don't need it no more. He's old and shit. Ow, Lee. Fuck..."

"Old men love sports cars," Richards opined.

"Not my old man. He loves kino and college boys," Mikey admitted.

"I see. Well then when you gettin' back?"

"Wednesday next week in the AM," Leanna informed him.

"Alright. We'll reconvene back here. With at least ten grand for yours truly. Yes?"

"Yeah. Fine."

"Anything extra will be considered a tip and greatly appreciated, of course."

A tip? I'll give you the whole fucking rod, shitbag.

Leanna slipped Richards a torn little piece of paper.

"The address. She should be back from Haiti any time now. And you can grab whatever you want from the house. She's got shit stashed all over. I'm sure you can make it worth your while. Make it look like a robbery and the such."

"Haiti? She into some voodoo shit or something?"

Leanna sighed and pursed her lips. Her mother was such a fucking embarrassing gimmick. Just hearing the word 'voodoo' all by its lonesome made her want to kill at random.

"Anything else?" She popped up to leave and Mikey followed suit.

"Depends, junebug. Anything else I need to know?"

"Yeah. Don't talk to her. Just kill her. She'll fuck with your head."

Richards didn't bother to respond, he simply stared down at his coffee and grunted as Mikey and Leanna left.

~666~

Leanna and Mikey burst out of the diner and hurried to the car. They piled in and sped off without a single look back at the Cluck Shack.

"Your mom's gonna be pissed when she figures out what you just done."

"Let her be. Won't be long after her epiphany she'll be dead."

"Well I kinda feel bad for her, in a manner of speaking."

"What was that? Mind repeating it for me?"

"Nothin'."

"How much cash you got left?"

"I got another five grand, but that's everything, Lee."

"That should get us to Arizona easy."

"What about back here?"

"We ain't never coming back to this shithole, baby."

"What about that parole officer? What about the fucking hitman we just hired? Everybody thinks we're coming back."

"I know."

"Are you crazy? What if this drug guy decides not to pay us?"

"How many guns you bring?"

"Both shotguns, my .45 and a couple .38's. Why?"

Leanna rubbed on Mikey's crotch. She knew how to hit the sweet spot in less than five seconds. Soon, the stiffening unmistakable. Mikey groaned in pleasure but continued with his panicked realization.

"This is some serious shit you're stirring up. I thought it was just gonna be a quick run out west and back."

"There's something else."

"Oh no. What?"

"When I went over to her house, Ronnie was there."

"McGiffin?"

"No, country and western legend Ronnie Millsap paid me a visit. The fuck?"

"Well, what about him?"

Leanna rubbed Mikey's cock bulge even more vigorously, reaching for his zipper.

"What about him, Lee?"

"I, uh, I think I killed him."

"You think? Shit-shit-shit. Maybe he's still alive."

"I strangled him till his neck snapped. Now that I think about it, he's definitely dead. Besides, he's the one who done turned me in. Fuck him and his midget fetish."

"Oh my Jesus!"

"Calm down, babe. Let Lee release some of that pressure."

She reached in through his zipper hole and grabbed ahold of Mikey Junior.

"There he is," she smirked.

"The cops'll be after us faster than we can split. Oh lord this is it. Jesus take the wheel."

"Don't worry. She ain't calling no cops. She's gonna wanna get even with us on her own. And she ain't gonna get a chance to do that once Ricky gets done with her."

"Lee... I... I don't know if I can do all this. I—"

Mikey cried the tears of a scared little boy. Leanna stopped rubbing on Mikey, her tone changing drastically.

"Yeah, you can. What the fuck else are you gonna do? Everybody in this town thinks you're a fucking moron. Your dad hates your guts, and you barely snagged a GED. What are you gonna do here? Huh?"

"I thought you and me could—you think I'm uh...a moron, Lee?"

"No. I mean, you're a little slow, babe. But like with math and shit. So you're my kinda slow."

"You know I love you, right?"

"Yeah, I know. And there ain't no one else I'd wanna do this with."

Mikey leaned over to kiss Leanna. She put her hand back in his pants and gave him the old up-and-down.

"Eyes on the road, stud."

NINETEEN...

Teena felt much freer on this particular return to her house. No cab, no Leanna, no nonsense. Just a crystal-clear sense of purpose for once in her life. She led a gurgling, babbling Wallis by the hand inside, gently taking him to the front room. Ronnie was in there, standing still as a statue. One of his eyes bulged out slightly and his neck was a twisted mess. He'd already started to decay a little. Bits and bobs of him had dropped to the floor like so much melting ice cream. He stared blankly through the large window he found himself in front of even though it was covered by thick black curtains. The flummoxed idleness of the freshly dead. It fascinated Teena to no end.

To see what he sees. I wish I could.

"You're up! You look well, darling," Teena exclaimed with a soft clap of her hands.

Ronnie turned to look at Teena with a half grin, thick black sputum dribbling from his crooked mouth.

"Ronnie honey, I know you remember dear Wallis. Wallis, remember Ronnie? Small town and all, right boys?"

Teena laughed out loud to a captive audience of two and hugged Wallis, who groaned in exhaustion and also possibly out of love.

"You two have a lot to catch up on, I know you do."

Silence. The two bachelors locked eyes. Empty, dead peepers meeting one another by accident. Then, twitching away from each other to gawk at something else mindlessly.

"I've got some packing to do and then we'll be off, okay?"

Ronnie looked up at the ceiling, probably involuntarily, his neck cracking the entire way.

"It is so good to have you both here with me. After all this time. I should have done this sooner."

Wallis managed to move his head in the appropriate direction to look at Teena. He let out a shrill croak, causing a jet of dark green bile to shoot from his mouth in a short, sharp spurt.

"Well, I'm off then. I'll just be down the hall if you need me, my darlings. You two play nice now."

Wallis vomited again. Ronnie let out a dead, hollow laugh as some spew landed on his crooked shoulder.

~666~

Teena packed a travel bag full of clothes and a few strange vials. She stuffed her *Caplatas & Evil Intent* book in there as well. The low and slow hum she used to center and calm herself filled the bedroom with a false sense of security. Normalcy. But down the hall in the front room stood stark reality itself on four dead, decaying legs.

The packing helped her find equilibrium as much as the humming. *Finally, a break from the norm.* Whatever "the norm" was these days, of course. Teena deduced Leanna was most likely sheltering at Mikey's abode. But not for long. They'd want to get a move on after breaking and entering. And murder. At least Leanna would. Mikey was ever the unassuming accessory. People made fun of Wallis for being slow, but he never suffered from the moral indecision Mikey possessed whenever it came to the matter of Leanna. Could that be love? Real, living, breathing love? Knowing the one you love is rotten and loving them anyways? The idea that Mikey was somehow a better person for doing so compared to her was outrageous. She wouldn't entertain it for one second longer.

Her humming rose to a mild fever pitch, and she almost didn't notice the cock of the hammer of a gun behind her. She stopped harmonizing and tilted her head slightly.

"Close your eyes. Easier that way," Ricky's voice vibrated from somewhere behind her, most likely left of center. She could sense the barrel of the gun just millimeters from her hair. It gave her a tingling sensation she almost relished.

"I have some jewelry and cash in the other room if that's what you require," Teena said, calm as a warm bath.

"That is not what I require. What I require is for you to shut the fuck up and close your goddamned eyes." Richards spat as he spoke. Teena felt some of his spittle dab her hair. Was he getting flustered? Did Leanna believe she was hiring a professional? Always thinking she's one step ahead, that girl.

Teena turned to look at him and began humming again. Unafraid of the gun just inches from her face. The look on Richards's face spoke of slight hints of confusion and annoyance.

Not a music fan, I wager.

"Stop that," he blurted out.

Teena didn't stop.

"I said shut the fuck up and—"

Dead arms reached out and dead hands grabbed on to Richards. His gun went off and the bullet zinged past Teena's head, barely an inch away. She could feel the hot whiz of the round even after it was lodged in her bedroom wall. Wallis and Ronnie groaned angrily at Richards. Was that hunger? Or just blind obedience?

Richards was more than a little taken aback as he was restrained by the living dead. "What the fu—"

Teena moved closer to him, still humming. Wallis and Ronnie seemed to be entranced by the sound. They *were* entranced by the sound.

"She said you was fuckin' weird, but this takes the goddamn bizarro cake."

Teena laughed an annoying schoolgirl laugh. The kind that sounded like nails on a chalkboard to adults no longer privy to the joys of youth.

"How much did you get? I hope you know you won't be getting any more. She won't be back. Not for me, not for you. Not for anything in the world. Now put the gun down or join my flock, sweetie."

"Huh? Aw, fuck this."

Richards broke free from Wallis and Ronnie's grip and ran straight through the floor-to-ceiling window in between himself and Teena, just to their right, smithereening it in the process.

Gunshots rang out from outside the window and a handful of bullets struck Ronnie and Wallis in the chest and arms. Gish-gushes of black blood and viscera exploded from their grey and green skin onto the shag carpet. Not much effect beyond that. They both stared at the bullet holes curiously.

Teena peered through the shattered window and out into the emptiness of the night. She could hear faint, retreating footfalls. They were out of sync. He was injured. She chuckled a bit and inhaled the magic of the night air. Ronnie and Wallis finished inspecting their bullet wounds and started to lumber after their prey, but Teena stopped them from giving chase with a gentle hand on each one of their caved-in chests.

"Wait. Not yet, my lovelies. Let's get you cleaned up first."

~666~

All sliced up from the glass and with a twisted ankle, Richards yelped repeatedly as he limped and huffed his way through the darkness to his Buick, hidden just out of sight in the tree line surrounding Teena's property.

The fuck was that? What in the fumbling fuck was that?

As he flung open the door to his car, he whipped around to see if anyone or anything was following him. His ankle throbbed. Blood trickled into his eyes from a sizable cut on his forehead. He aimed and cocked his gun into the darkness of the woods, searching for any moving thing at all. Nothing. He wasn't followed. But why not? Those freaks should be on him by now. It bothered him more than he liked.

God damn glass. God damn motherfucking glass.

He dabbed his forehead with the sleeve of his jacket a few times, arm shaking from the adrenaline pumping in his veins.

"Fucking crazy bitches. Fuck this family feud."

He put his gun away and scanned the area one last time. Simultaneously hoping to see and not see something emerging from the pitch black surrounding him.

~666~

Richards drove at highly illegal speeds down the curvaceous one-lane blacktop leading back into town. He winced in full-bodied pain as he tried to call someone on his beige pre-paid flip phone.

"Answer the goddamn phone, Sharnell!"

Leanna, Leanna, oh boy do you got some 'splainin' to do. Think you can skip town and stiff me on the rest of the bill? And my tip? Fuck that shit sideways.

Someone answered and his tone changed from angrily frantic to frantically hopeful.

"Baby, listen... I know. I need you to... Well, that's not my fault. Look, will you just... I don't know how she knows that. She's fucking crazy... No, I don't want to fuck her. Why would you... Of course I love you. Yes... Yes... I said yes. Would you just listen to me for one second, please? I need you to find out who her parole officer is. Yeah, I know that's gonna be hard, that's why I'm asking you. Just call me when you find out. Okay... Okay... I said okay! I love you too. Bye."

Richards hung up and immediately dialed another number as he whined in frustration and hurt. Lots of naked, bare-assed hurt.

PART THREE

ROAD GAMES

Dear Fucking Diary,

I asked the bitch if she was working over my man. The fucking way she said no made me want to goddamn puke. Then I asked Mikey point blank if he was fucking Teena. Or if Teena was fucking him. He said no way. Sounded hurt I would even ask. I believe him. I don't believe her. If you know what I mean.

-LF

TWENTY...

The incessant vibrations from Mikey's Trans Am usually irked the shit out of Leanna, but tonight they calmed her into a soothing pre-sleep stupor. She was free and Teena was about to pay for it all. There was nothing left to stew about. At least for a few hundred miles. Sleep sounded like the perfect drug for the night.

As she drifted off, an involuntary thought of Ronnie swept across her brain. Was it guilt? Or was it just a remnant of the past letting off its last pitiful death rattle?

~666~

This had to be guilt. Remembering past events like they were dreams pissed off Leanna mightily. Try as hard as she could, she was unable wake up from this golden oldie.

Fuck.

Ronnie and Leanna were splayed out on the couch in Leanna's shitty old apartment, back when she was gainfully employed at the Birdcage Gentlemen's Lounge a few years ago. They were half-naked, smoking some of Jiman's weed on the couch. Purple People Eater. Made you hungry for Indian food. They looked like they just had sweaty movie star sex.

I think that was the time we tried to play the Blindfold Game under the bed. The night we decided to go steady. Or some such thing.

"We're gonna be in so much trouble, Lee. You know that, right?"

"Says who? She don't need to know. And she won't unless someone tells her. Right?"

Ronnie took a long drag off his joint and remained silent. Leanna punched him in the arm, causing him to exhale sharply. Smoke billowed all around her unsmiling face.

"Sorry. Right. I won't say anything. I promise."

More quiet. Just inhales and exhales. The rhythm of post-coitus recuperation.

"You know what that means, right?" He braced for another possible punch.

"What?"

"I still have to see her. Keep up appearances."

"Uh-uh. Just dump her."

No punch came. She was surprisingly unviolent in her reaction.

"Then she'll really be suspicious. Besides, staying with her will give us a good excuse to be around each other," Ronnie reasoned.

"You're not gonna have your cake and eat it too. Ace her and we'll figure out something as we go." Leanna folded her arms. That usually meant negotiations were over.

"Brilliant. Why didn't I think of that?"

The second punch came when Ronnie wasn't expecting it. Right in the ribs.

"Fuck off. I'm not sharing you with her. It's all or nothing," she nearly screeched. Leanna then jumped on Ronnie and kissed him aggressively. Lips pressing hard into his, equally arousing and uncomfortable.

"You hear me?" she asked as she came up for air.

"I hear you, baby. Loud and clear." Ronnie stared into her eyes as he almost stammered his words. Whether it was from infatuation or intimidation was unclear.

~666~

Leanna woke from her rough sleep. Mikey chuckled and rubbed her thigh. A highway sign passed them on the right. Leanna's eyes were too bleary to see it clearly, but she knew she wanted to stop somewhere. And soon.

"You alright? You were mumbling something fierce."

"Yeah, yeah. Just a dumb dream."

"Was I in it?"

"No. And you wouldn't wanna be. Trust me."

"That bad, huh?"

They passed another highway sign. This time Leanna could see food, gas, and lodging advertised. The car grew quiet; as if the inevitable events of the immediate future had settled in the back seat and were leering at them with bloody, cancerous eyes. Leanna tried to think of a joke but was coming up zeroes.

"You got any good memories of your daddy?" Mikey broke that silence with the most innocent, inquisitive tone an adult who seen some depressing shit could possibly muster,

She did, though. A good handful of them. One she always went back to was when her dad took her to the pro-wrestling matches at the Bayfront Plaza. He was so excited to share something with her that she could feel it. Literally feel it. Even back then at that age. She didn't remember anything about the show, just how it all felt. The roar of the crowd, the hot dog she had. Extra ketchup. She could still smell his aftershave. CK One. Regardless of whether it was a proper memory or not, it was the one she always came back to when things were quiet.

"Nah, not really," she replied.

"Me neither."

The silence returned for a moment. It felt disingenuous. She had to nip it in the bud.

"So where we at?" she asked, looking for another road sign of any import.

"Oh, 'bout halfway to El Paso. Fort Stockton comin' up. Ain't nothin' but good ol' I-10 from here 'til Arizona. Easy peasy. You wanna drive?"

"Later. Still tired as shit. When are we stopping?"

"Figured somewhere around El Paso. Cheap motels and the such."

"I gotta pee. Stop at the next place."

"You got it, missy."

Mikey's car veered off the highway onto the next exit toward a skeezy, half-lit truck stop gas station adorned by a Mexican restaurant that was either closed or out of business and an all-night convenience store. Leanna tried to think of the look on her mother's face when Ricky Richards caught up with her. To her dismay, she couldn't quite picture it. Something wasn't clicking. Teena's visage wouldn't come into focus. Maybe it was due to lack of sleep. More importantly, she had to pee and grab a drink. Maybe then she could fantasize about her mother's death the proper way.

TWENTY-ONE...

Stubborn bitch. How the fuck did Forsythe crack her?

Ricky Richards enjoyed ransacking Marion Killford's office even though it already looked like she lived in it and the maid killed herself at least five years ago. *In* the office.

He searched the place top to bottom for any sign of Leanna's whereabouts and even asked her parole officer nicely. He hardly ever did that. That's how bad he wanted to "catch up" with that treacherous skank.

Killford was handcuffed with her arms behind her back in her office chair. On top of that, her arms were tied to the chair itself with fishing wire. Criss-crossed lines of blood seeped through the wire with her every move. Her face was a handful of punches away from ground beef. The eighty-seven percent lean kind.

Richards took a bottle of half-drunk top-shelf whiskey off her desk and poured it on his bloody knuckles. Then he splashed it on his sliced-up face and arms, courtesy of Teena's big-ass bedroom window. It hurt so good and burned away the stench of those crazy fucks who tried to hold him down.

"Mmmm-hmm. Hate to waste good hooch, but—"

"It's worthless once it touches your hayseed hands," she muttered at him, spitting blood at the same time.

Richards punched her right in the face hard and quick. He felt one of his knuckles pop on her cheekbone. *Fuck.* Killford let out a slight wheeze but nothing more. She was tough; he'd give her that.

"Where'd you get all that cut-up lovin'? You got a window shopping fetish? Or did some saint of a woman finally give you what for?"

This smartass clit connoisseur ain't gonna last much longer than a mayfly's honeymoon, I wager.

"Hardy fucking har. Just tell me where she's headed and the route thereabouts and we can go grab some flapjacks and have a few laughs. My treat."

Killford hocked a glob of blood on the floor directly in front of Richards.

"Clean that up before you leave," she whispered, her resolve almost spent.

Richards chortled through his crooked teeth and took a swig of whiskey. "Guess I'm gonna have to flip my switch from interrogation to penetration."

Killford's eyes widened just enough. Poker face broken. Richards knew he was on the verge of information paydirt and prepared to relish these final moments.

"I'm gonna do my best impression of the Little Dutch Boy. 'Cept I ain't gonna use my finger."

He placed the whiskey back on the table and pulled out his .38 revolver, aiming it square at Killford's head while he loosened her arms from the chair with his boot knife and then threw her to the ground without the slightest ounce of care.

"Assume the position, baby."

He forced her on her stomach and undid his acid wash jeans, dropping them to his knees. He'd never tried this on a dyed-in-the-wool bull before. It made him pause for just a moment.

Will my pecker work? Does it even matter?

"Last chance before magic time, honey."

"Go to hell, hillbilly."

"Oh dear. And it's all boos from the crowd."

Richards reached down to pull off her pants and that's when she mule kicked him hard and sent him reeling backwards. He rolled his hurt ankle again and cursed a blue streak as he tried to regain his footing.

Moving like a frantic, wounded rabbit, Killford managed to get upright and on her feet, using her desk for support. Her hands were still handcuffed behind her back but that didn't seem to slow her down.

"Ah, I see where this is going." Richards put up his dukes playfully. An itty-bitty old fist fight couldn't hurt. But just a little one. Time was a-wasting.

Instead of swinging at him, Killford charged him, slamming him up against the wall. As he tried to catch his breath, she quickly headbutted him, breaking his nose. Blood gushed from it freely. He hadn't felt this kind of a rush from such sudden and resolute resistance since his bounty hunter days. It would have excited him immensely if his nose wasn't leaking like a faucet and his ankle felt like it was about to fall off.

"Stand still so I can beat the fucking shit of ya, you ugly ass—"

Richards barely managed to utter that string of words through his mess of a face before Killford rushed him again only to be stopped by a vicious clothesline from Richards.

Not this time, bitch.

"Fool me once…"

She writhed in pain on the floor as Richards ripped her pants and underwear off. His gun in one hand while the other hand grasped her neck tightly.

"You gonna talk? What do ya owe that gash anyway? She played you like she played me. Say somethin' worthwhile or we're gonna play a game of reverse whack-a-mole!"

Killford's demeanor finally broke. She sobbed loudly before screaming uncontrollably.

"You think I like this shit? Stop making me do this to you! Where the fuck is that deceitful little whore headed to?"

Through her defeated sobbing, she finally uttered a single word clearly.

"Tucson…"

If they're going where I think… Crafty bitch. Crafty-ass bitch.

Richards kicked her flat to the ground.

"No fibbing, now."

"She's going to Tucson. I-10 all the way. Got her boyfriend with her."

"They packing?"

"Hope so…"

BLAM! Richards yanked the trigger, sending a bullet right into the small of her back. She whimpered in agony, ejecting little puffs of breath with a soft moan.

"Stupid twat. Hope so? Fuck you."

He ripped her shirt off her body and used it to wipe the thick smear of blood from his face. He touched his nose with the tip of his finger and winced. *Definitely fucking broken.* With his free hand, Richards made a call. He clicked his tongue while he waited for someone to pick up. Killford moaned a low, quiet rumble of agony and humiliation. She was still hanging in there after all that.

Fucking unbelievable. Resilient piece of—

Someone on the other end answered his call. "Yeah... You were right on the money. Killford in the flesh. No, still alive. But I don't think she's gonna be walking to no rug buffets anytime soon. Wheels all the way... No, I'll call it in. Make it look like that tricky bitch and her shithead walking penis of a boyfriend fucked her up. Disgruntled parolee and what have you. They're headed to Tucson... Oh, I know. Drakesworth's turf. Pack what you need and get ahead of 'em. I'll bring up the rear. There's more to this shit than meets the ever-lovin' eye..."

He hung his phone up and scanned the floor for something. It took him a minute, but he soon found Killford's own phone next to a half-drunk can of Milwaukee's Best.

Hello there.

He snatched up her errant phone and dialed a three-digit number. As he spoke, he tried to mimic a young twentysomething female as best he could. It sounded more like mockery than mimicry.

"Hello? Yes, something awful's just happened. My parole officer's been shot. It's terrible, I can't... Who shot her? Well, I did. That's why I'm calling... Well I still feel bad about it, for Christ's sake... Why did I do it? Who gives a fuck? She's a stupid bitch and so am I! Just get over here and arrest me. Leanna Forsythe. Yeah... I'll be waiting for ya, kay?"

Richards hung up and chortled. When they show up and Leanna's nowhere to be found, the biggest manhunt this side of the

Gulf Coast will commence, leaving local law dogs busy looking for a needle that's not there in a haystack that no one gives a shit about.

Job well done, Richards. Time for a cold one.

Ricky looked for an unopened beer amidst the ruins of his fight with Killford. He found one tucked up underneath her office chair.

Natty Light. Might as well piss in my own mouth.

As he popped the top, he glanced over at Killford. She was still face down and barely breathing. Richards was nearing gobsmackery at the fact she was still alive.

"This one's for you. And I ain't heard a thank you yet for savin' yer life."

Richards toasted Killford and swigged the shitty beer down. Sirens would sound out soon. It was time to skedaddle.

"Don't you worry none, I'll find little Leanna for ya. Ain't nothin' but a thing."

Ricky Richards' kingly curiosity as to what the fuck was really going on with this insane mother/daughter pairing was outmatched only by his greed. He could smell a proper, big-ass payday hiding somewhere in plain sight. Wherever Leanna was going, the *real* money lurked and that made him hard as fuck.

TWENTY-
TWO...

As Zebulon Carruthers finished hitching Teena's old horse trailer to her little red Nissan pickup truck, she looked to the moon. A crescent-looking fellow hanging out up there, sitting in judgment of everyone. Especially her.

Zeb was her nearest neighbor. Nearest meant about a mile up the road and she liked it that way. Privacy was a valuable commodity. Especially during her marathon late night screaming matches with Leanna.

He was decrepit, but in a sweet, unassuming way. As a matter of fact, Zeb was the only man Teena had been able to trust for nearly twenty years. It wasn't on account of not trying, that's for damn sure.

She threw her bags into her car right as Zeb finished connecting the truck to the trailer. He wasted no time returning to an upright position, albeit slowly.

"Welp. That'll do 'er, Miss Forsythe."

"Zeb. You angel. Again, thank you for coming over so late. I can't tell you how much of an emergency this is," Teena confessed as she approached him.

He took off his faded ballcap and dusted off his tattered overalls with it. A bashful smile crept across his crinkled lips as he did so.

"Aw, well I ain't had nothing else to do no-how, on account of my insomnia. I was just watching that show where they open up suitcases and find all kinds of crazy doodads. Ya think that stuff's on the up and up?"

Teena handed him a folded Post-It note with a soft flourish of her hand. "Here's where I'm headed for a few days. Let me know if we get any visitors, okay? I will forever be in your debt, sweetie."

Zeb opened the note and eyeballed it for a second.

"Austin? Shoot, won't catch me headed there no time soon. You watch out for them hippies now, ya hear?"

Teena giggled and gave him a soft kiss on his cheek. It almost bowled him over right onto his breakable ass.

"You sure it's gonna fit both of 'em, uh, *horses*? Should only be for one, I reckon."

"They're quite...flexible. This will do just fine."

"Well, I'll be monkey-uncled. You sure are full o' surprises, Miss Forsythe. What'll you think of next?"

"Thank you, dear Zeb. Goodnight."

"Night, darlin'."

Zeb did his best impression of human molasses and oozed back into his ancient pickup truck. It ambled down Teena's driveway as slow as he was old. As soon as he was out of sight, she looked back to her house, smiled, and hummed that same eerie tune again.

TWENTY-
THREE...

R icky Richards' apartment had never seen better days in its entire sad-ass life. It was always firmly in the shithole category. The sheer musk of lingering cigarette funk enveloped everything within. Old gun and muscle car magazines covered most pieces of furniture along with random assortments of half-empty beer cans of the Busch and Keystone family trees. David Allan Coe warbled his way through the apartment from a record player on the tobacco-stained Formica kitchen bar top.

In his bedroom, Richards was splayed out ass up, completely naked on his ratty queen bed, the sheets dingy with Essence of Pall Mall. His skin looked like an angular jigsaw puzzle courtesy of Teena's window. Sharnell had cleaned every slit and gash up with alcohol and cotton swabs. Pain before pleasure tonight. She now stood over him, as if she had just gotten up off him. She too was naked, and her medium-sized cock was still half-hard and glistened with lube and her own cum in the dim yellow lamp light of her lover's bed chambers. She was toned and tan with just barely defined abs and an emerald belly ring Ricky loved sucking on. Her raven hair bubbled up and overflowed in the thick grey scrunchy she used to tie it up with before Ricky swooped in on her.

Richards swiped a dented cigarette from his nightstand and lit it with the discerning care of a cigar afficionado.

Not one glob of shit on that glorious hog of hers. Fuck, that was great.

"I don't wanna do this no more," Sharnell half-whispered. The exhaustion in her voice made Ricky grimace as she folded her arms. Ricky knew exactly what she meant, but he was never one for the direct approach. He knew this day was coming for a long time. It didn't make it any less annoying for him, though.

"Them blue pills fucking with your equilibrium again? Ya gotta drink more water before we—"

"You know what I mean, pendejo. I told you there was only a few more left on your punch card. Now the card's all punched out."

Ricky flipped over with a wry smile. His baby python cock flopped to one side with a subtle thud of gristly meat. Sharnell wasn't in the mood to bottom so she compromised and blew him proper. It was a top twenty blowjob of recent memory. He made a note to tell her just that after this particular exchange subsided. Even when an argument was brewing, Ricky felt it was always more on the verge of a flirt session with her.

"Yeah but don't that mean I get a free one?" He clicked his tongue and winked at her.

"That *was* your free one. You got it? I can't..."

Ricky's face drooped.

Aw hell and goddamn it all to it.

"Look, c'mere baby. I get it. It's time. I know it is."

He grabbed her and sucked her into his playful embrace with squeeze and a chuckle. She smiled and he had her again.

"You make your appointment yet? The, uh con-sul-tation, I mean. Right?"

She nodded, sniffing involuntarily.

"I'll be there," he muttered.

"You promise? No fucking around this time, Ricky."

"None whatsoever. I promise. Honest cracker."

She kissed him and he knew she knew he was telling the truth. He gave her that deep, lip-squishing kiss that meant he meant business. Whatever that business might entail.

It was time to hit the road, though. No room for seconds.

"Thanks for the patch job."

"But it's time to bounty hunt a bitch," she said as she finished his thought.

"Shit. At least two." He flashed her a pair of knuckly fingers as smoke oozed out of his nose.

"You think she really set you up? With those...*things* back there?"

"Probably not. But at this juncture, I don't give a damn either way. Them two syphilitic vultures got a blood feud between 'em and they don't give a good green grocer's care at all about who they use to fuck each other over. Besides, why would she have anything against little old me? Figure it was an honest hit for honest pay and the stupid bitch had no idea Mommy was into crackheads now. That means she and her idiot boy toy were in a big, sloppy ass hurry to leave. Probably some dead bodies lying around to boot. And *that* means there's really something else going on entirely. Something big. Something nigh invaluable. And that's where we come in.

Officially. *I. Want. My. Fucking. Money.* Even if I gotta kill the ever-lovin' Kingpin of the Southwest to get it."

"Hey, the fucking money is *all* that matters; we gotta remember that. Running around killing everyone involved even tangentially sounds fun, yeah, but that shit is complicated to get clear of. Know what I'm sayin' baby?"

"Oh, I hear you mamacita. One thing's for sure, though. Miss Leanna's gonna cough up whatever she's got and then some before she chokes to death...on my dick."

"You do got a way with words. Glad we're on the same team, lover."

"Couldn't do it without ya, mama. No way, no how. Ain't foolin'."

"My man." Sharnell smiled. She went in to kiss him again, mimicking his prior aplomb.

"That's me," he muttered and moaned betwixt her lips.

Yeah, that's me.

Sharnell pulled away from their kiss, remembering something with a brittle snap of her fingers.

"Almost forgot, baby. Got two dudes you should talk to. They're good at tying up loose ends and shit. And it sounds like our loose ends punch card is all full up."

Ricky frowned at the term loose ends. She was right, though. Loose ends aplenty right about now. These guys she was talking about better not be more of her boneheaded prison buddies.

Great. This should be inter-fucking-resting right down to the son of a bitching ground.

"Can they tie a motherfuckin' Palomar knot 'round the loose ends we got?"

TWENTY-
FOUR...

Jiman's flesh smelled like stale weed and regurgitated Taco Bell. Ronnie and Wallis didn't seem to mind, though. Teena would have gagged were it not for the other aroma she detected.

Lilacs and blood.

A small mountain of it in his system. They could have just waited around in his cramped studio loft for him to drop dead on account of the dust shutting down every organ in his wiry frame sooner rather than later. It wasn't meant for such fast, hard, and repeated consumption. She had told Leanna that much the last time she tried to steal it. Unsuccessfully. Her first date with Mikey. Wanted to impress him. She wondered if Leanna and Mikey had taken as much as Jiman here. Would her work be done before it even started?

No. Not yet. Not like that.

Leanna may have been more impulsive than the combined hormones of a junior prom, but she was not stupid. She'd dole it out at the right time. Special occasions. Certain public exhibitions. This would be a long chase filled with more than a few bodies.

Teena said a short, solemn prayer for those soon to be killed at the hands of her own daughter.

She drifted back to reality just as Ronnie and Wallis finished eating out Jiman's chest cavity. Ravioli-sized chunks of his intestines dotted the floor around his carcass. She couldn't tell which pieces of his gut were oozing food and which were oozing shit. His face was locked in a look of both surprise and disappointment. Another idiot lowlife dead at the indirect hands of Leanna. His gold teeth clenched to the point of breaking when Ronnie had bitten through his navel just moments ago. That's when he screamed out just two words.

Tucson. Drakesworth.

Teena flinched when she heard that name. She knew it well. Well enough, at least. The parties she and Derek had under the alluring thumb of the dust and its influence attracted all kinds of merrymakers. Pimps, porn stars, local politicians, and of course drug dealers. Drakesworth was small time back then. Jiman-level small time. But she heard he had grown into something big and fierce further out west. Arizona, she had heard. Teena was just glad he was removed from Texas. He would tell the foulest stories of true death and corruption whenever he showed up to one of their parties. Derek loved hearing them, but they unnerved Teena. They didn't feel like stories. More like life goals. Dreams and expectations he was hoping to achieve. Most people would tell these kinds of stories aghast, hoping to get a reaction out of their audience. A cautionary tale to remain square and safe and out of the gaze of the unsavory. With Drakesworth, though, Teena felt he admired the perpetrators in these stories. Revered them. Maybe he was hoping to recruit some who heard them to his cause. Whatever he did in those ensuing years must have worked. He must have set himself up in Tucson, most likely surrounded by the death and corruption he so very much wanted all those years ago.

When Derek died, the dust went away. The parties stopped. The ne'er do wells vanished. All went silent. Except for the fights with Leanna as she grew up and into a more violent, insistent version of Derek. She never thought anything like that was possible. But there she was, walking, talking, breathing, screaming, fucking, and judging. Just existing in the same space with her felt like living with a parasite-by-proxy, an entity that just kept taking and taking and taking and asking for more and insulting you with the vilest of accusations all the while.

She'll know the truth soon.

There was also the matter of that disgusting hitman. Would that be another inconvenience she must suffer through? When will it end? Will it all go away if Leanna...

She stopped herself from even thinking it. She had to get the dust out of her hands above all else.

But if that meant she had to—

Della would know what to do. She'd say it right away.

There was no avoiding it. The city limits of Austin would have to be her next stop. Leanna and Mikey were already too far ahead to catch up to them tonight. They'd soon stop for a vulgar display of affection. Somewhere big. Somewhere offensive. It was inevitable. Teena had time. She *needed* Della. It was decided.

"The shadows will find us soon. We must away. Now," she explained to her undead lovers, as if they understood what that meant.

She hummed softly and yanked on Wallis and Ronnie's chains for them to finish up and prepare to leave, not sure if she should be worried for Leanna or for Drakesworth.

TWENTY-FIVE...

Leanna leaned on Mikey's car without an immediate care in the world. She had changed into a halter top, cutoff short shorts, and flip flops. She was sweaty from being plastered to the leather passenger seat in Mikey's car during her slumber and was enjoying the cool Central Texas night air. As cool as it could be, that is. Mikey refused to crank the air past a slight breeze no matter how much she protested. She chugged a forty of Miller High Life like it was water as she people-watched.

A young couple in their twenties walked by. Gaged ears, matching wolf t-shirts. Probably looking to peruse the Monster section of the drink aisle. The guy got more than a quick look at Leanna, and his girlfriend let him know about it.

"Twenty to touch it, fifty to suck it," Leanna said matter-of-factly, knowing exactly how this would play out.

The guy stopped altogether and looked back at Leanna like a horny deer in headlights. How could anyone not? His girl screamed at him this time, smacking him about the body. They moved on after a moment. Leanna smiled.

"Hundred to fuck it."

Mikey stumbled out of the truck stop store and bumped into the warring couple. He had an armful of dumbass junk food in tow. Cheese puffs, cupcakes, energy drinks, candy bars. You name it.

"Anything for me?"

"You like Choco-Tooties?"

"How old are you?"

"Old enough to ride you, little girl."

"If I didn't already know you, I'd call the fucking cops."

"I bet that's a compliment somewhere."

As they were just about to get back in the car, two men dressed in dark clothes and big hats approached them on either side. One had a gun, the other a knife. The guy with the gun was muscular and scarred, from what she could see through his clothes. The guy with the knife had a large tattoo of a severed head on his cheek and was very skinny. Almost too skinny. It creeped Leanna out more than she liked.

"Hands in the air, newlyweds," the guy with the gun said.

"And wave them like you actually do care," the guy with the knife said.

"What the fuck is this? Who the fuck are you guys?"

"Lee—" Mikey looked like a scared chicken about to lay an egg just as the fox had wandered into the henhouse. He was not in his element and Leanna's mama bear instincts were about to kick in even while her mouth insisted on digging their grave deeper and deeper.

"I'm Dierks and this is my business associate Flavio. Mr. Drakesworth sends his regards. That good enough for you to get mugged now, sweetie?"

Fucking Drakesworth? Okay then, asshole...

The guy with the gun looked and sounded like the leader of the two, Leanna wagered. Time to get him all riled up. At least, that was the plan she came up with in about twenty seconds. It was as good as any other at this point in the game.

"Are you fucking kidding me right now? Are those your stripper names or your porn names?" Leanna asked as she folded her arms and snorted.

Dierks balked but recovered by taking a few steps closer to Leanna, inserting his gun directly into her immediate facial space. "The hell is wrong with our names? And you won't live long enough to know for sure if you don't shut your trap-ass mouth. Now, your cash and anything else useful. Let's go."

"But first you need to pull around back. Get in," Flavio mumbled. He could be the wild card in the equation, Leanna realized. Dierks talked, Flavio killed. People with knives were usually much crazier than those with guns in her experiences so far in life. She preferred a knife, too. So there was that.

There was nothing for it. If she was going to get the jump on these two dipshits, it was time to play along for at least a little while. So Mikey and Leanna reluctantly got in the front as Dierks and Flavio got in the back. Mikey drove the car around to the rear of the truck stop at a snail's pace. Maybe he was hoping there'd be somebody around to alert the police. But there was no one. She admired his thinking, but it was going to take more than a weak S.O.S. to unfuck this fuckery. The car pulled up next to a dumpster and away from anyone within earshot. A dirty, flickering light on the wall of the building cast a weird shadow.

Mood lighting. I like it.

"Get out," Dierks barked.

"Now," Flavio whispered.

"You fuckers have no idea who you're—"

Dierks whacked Mikey on the head with the butt of his gun. Flavio brandished his blade in front of Leanna. "The fuck did we just say? Move it."

Mikey rubbed his head as he got out of the car slowly. Leanna jumped out in a huff, cursing under her breath.

"Your woman's a real uppity cunt, kid," Dierks asserted.

"You got no idea, mister."

"Hand over your cash. Pronto." Flavio looked eager to use his knife on someone. Anyone.

Mikey pulled out the wad of cash from his shorts and gave it to Dierks.

"How much?" Flavio asked with a flick of his wrist, causing his blade to gleam in the moonlight.

"It's, uh five grand. That's all we got."

Flavio stared down Mikey's fist wad and then his eyes floated over to the vicinity of the Trans Am's trunk. "Shit. That much green means there's something else in there. Open it up. We need a peek."

Fucking unbelievable. Leanna's notoriously short patience meter was already depleted. They were not getting in that trunk. "You got the cash, now fuck off."

Mikey moved closer to Dierks, hands out and pleading. "You guys should just leave—"

Dierks hit Mikey in the face with his gun, sending him to the ground with a surprised whimper.

"Who the fuck's robbing who here?" Flavio asked, frustration getting the better of him.

"These two ain't too bright. Pop the trunk and let's see what they got." Dierks wasn't budging on the trunk idea. It was sending

Leanna into more and more of a rolling boil with every second that passed.

"You don't wanna do that," she warned.

Dierks reached into the car and popped the trunk with a whistle. "Too late."

Mikey groaned, floundering in pain.

"Shut the fuck up," Flavio almost shouted. He was ready to stab. Leanna could smell it.

Dierks and Flavio went around to the trunk to have a look.

"Wait!"

They both turned to look at her, stopping just short of the trunk.

"What's it gonna take to make friends with you two?" Leanna asked. She was out of options. It was time to lean on the Old Faithful of diversion tactics.

"The fuck?" Dierks was legitimately flummoxed.

"She's screwin' with us. We should just off 'em and stash the car," Flavio grunted.

"I mean, what's it gonna take to make you happy? You know..." Leanna pulled up her shirt a little and her shorts down a little, revealing the bottoms of her breasts and just a wink of her manicured pubic hair.

"Oh," was all Flavio could say.

"That reminds me of a funny story. We're not into that kind of thing," Dierks confessed.

"The fuck you aren't." Leanna was determined to make this work. She couldn't imagine a world in which someone—anyone— had zero interest in her sexual wares.

"The fuck we ain't," Dierks reaffirmed.

Flavio looked over at Mikey pretty much involuntarily. Leanna caught it with a laser sharp twitch of her eye and struggled to contain an ear-to-ear grin.

"Ah. I see. An open relationship for you two?" she asked, hands on her hips.

"You could say that. Now shut your mouth and stay put and we just might let you live, sister." Dierks was near Flavio's level of annoyance and anger. It was now or never.

"You want him to take care of you guys?" Leanna said with an extreme helping of nonchalant matter-of-factness.

Mikey was back up on his feet just in time for his eyes to go wide. "Lee, what the hell—"

The two thieves exchanged a look.

"Is he up for it?" Now Flavio let his excitement at the possibilities show just a bit.

"Doesn't look like it," Dierks said with a shrug.

"Sure he is!" Leanna stared down Mikey, trying to will him to agree.

Mikey was seven different shades of red and that wasn't counting the blood from getting pistol-whipped. "I'm not—"

"Just do it, Mikey. Ain't no one gonna know."

"No pressure or nothing, kid." Dierks smiled politely as he helped Mikey up.

"Of course," Leanna said, super polite. Then she turned to Mikey and her smile faded. "You gotta do it, Mikey."

"No. I can't. I mean I don't know how." He was right on the verge of tears.

"It's easy. Just wrap your lips around it and suck."

"Like a lollipop. Or a popsicle," Flavio added, trying to seal the deal. What if Mikey hated popsicles and lollipops? Leanna couldn't remember him eating either one at any stage of their relationship. Her death tonight might start with a shitty blowjob, and it wouldn't be her fault.

Leanna patted Mikey on the back. "Whatever you prefer, baby. It can be a cigar. Or one of them whistle pops."

"Now you got us all riled up. No turning back," Dierks nearly squealed as he adjusted his bulge.

"Yeah, no choice now. On your knees, fella." Flavio was checking on his own tented crotch.

Mikey began to full-on ugly cry. She knew this was further than he'd ever been taken on one of her escapades and under normal circumstances she would sympathize in a heartbeat. But they were in a hurry and sympathy was an unwelcome neighbor at this hour of the night. Leanna brought her arm around from behind his back and slapped him hard.

"Man the fuck up and suck their dicks."

She leaned in so she could whisper something else to him. "We can't let them see inside that trunk. Not with the dust in there."

Mikey wiped a passel of tears from his raw, red cheek.

"Is this gonna make me queer, Lee?"

"No, babe. Only if you like it."

"Gospel." Dierks pumped his fist in agreement.

"Truth," Flavio muttered and nodded.

The two thieves undid their pants and dropped them, dicks out and ready. Dierks sported a stubby chubby that was much thicker than it would ever be wide. Flavio's was long and reverse telescoped, like a lumpy and bumpy peeled carrot. The pungent aroma of their combined dick cheese wafted into Mikey and Leanna's nostrils. Leanna was used to such smells and merely half-frowned but the smell made Mikey gag as he walked over to the now pantsless assailants with his head hung low, a light sob escaping him as he knelt in front of them.

"Jerk one of 'em off while you suck on one of 'em. Just like in the pornos, Mikey. 'Cept instead of a hot chick, it's you."

Mikey winced as he held Flavio's dick in his hand and reached out for Dierks' member, mouth opening slowly.

Leanna scooted over and onto the hood of the car, next to the passenger door. Distraction activated. It was now time to get into position, as it were.

"You mind if I take care of myself? This is kinda hot."

"Go for it."

Leanna put a hand down her shorts and went through the motions of massaging her clit, moaning a little too excessively to begin things.

Bring it down, bitch. Now's not the time to go all Meg Ryan on these fucks.

Mikey finally took Dierks' ballooning thumb-dick in his mouth as he stroked off Flavio, who was much bigger (and crookeder) compared to Dierks, whimpering about it all the way.

"Ain't this nice?" Flavio asked Dierks.

"Indeed. The very lap of luxury." Dierks looked down at Mikey and patted him on the head. "You're doing good, kid."

Mikey seemed to be doing a better job than Leanna had ever thought he could. Dierks and Flavio looked like they were in the throes of deep ecstasy as their heads went back and their eyes closed while Mikey bobbed on Dierks' cock with lips tightly covering his teeth as he stroked off Flavio, occasionally stopping to spit on Flavio's dick to keep the handjob nice and friendly.

And then Leanna felt something herself. Pleasure.

The fuck?

Being free and open in the night air and watching Mikey take on two guys at once was something Leanna apparently wanted to see for some reason. News to her. The sensation spread from her vaginal area to her thighs, radiating intensely.

Fuck this is good. Shit. Focus. You can do this.

There was still a job to do regardless of how good it felt. Her moans were genuine by now and she continued to masturbate with one hand as she reached into the car and into the glove box with her other hand and pulled out a .45 handgun. She knew all of Mikey's hiding places for guns. And condoms. Still moaning, it was all she could do to muster the energy not being spent on pleasuring herself to take aim at Dierks. She soon fired at him, slamming a bullet right into his chest. Dierks dropped his gun and fell backwards, dick sliding out of Mikey's mouth with a loud, wet POP.

With a wild, mournful scream, Flavio went for Leanna and tried to stab at her, but she shot him in the head just as he made it over to her. He fell on top of Leanna in a dead and still fully erect heap. A glob of his brain had smashed into Mikey's spiked hair and dented it considerably. Mikey plummeted into stunned silence, a trickle of drool running down his chin as he fell onto his butt.

I'm not finished. Fuck it.

She was close. Mikey had got her near enough she could take care of it on her own. She had found just the right groove and rubbed her index and middle fingers in precise rhythm back and forth over her clit. Soon after Dierks had expired from his sucking chest wound, Leanna finally climaxed, pushing Flavio off her as she bleated like a psychotic goat in the throes of a blunt and forceful orgasm. She wiped Flavio's headshot blood from her face as she tried to catch her breath, punching the car's hood with an adrenaline-fueled fist.

"I said goddamn. That's what that shit-eatin' Drakesworth gets for gettin' all impatient on us and shit."

"Lee, what the—"

"You done good, baby. Color me impressed. Fuck, that was good."

"Did... Did you just cum after you killed them guys?"

"Uh-huh."

"Why?"

"Cuz I already started beforehand, silly."

"But Lee—"

"It was actually kinda hot watching you switch teams. We should try that again some time. Under less stressful circumstances, of course."

"I need a shower. And unconsciousness."

"Oh, don't be so *hard* on yourself. You're a switch hitter if I ever saw one."

Leanna chuckled at her 'hard' joke as she grabbed one of the bodies and rolled it off to the side. Mikey grabbed the money and Leanna grabbed the gun and knife from Flavio and Dierks and without another word said between the two, they piled into the car and sped off.

~666~

Mikey concentrated on driving hard and fast, refusing to look at Leanna for anything.

"By the way, you get hard back there?" Leanna asked, a mischievous smile all about her.

"No. And why does it even matter? Jesus, Lee..."

"Just adding details to this scenario for my spank bank, baby. Research, if you will."

She cackled through her open window. A mating call for other psychos and savages that might be out there listening for their own kind.

Mikey just shook his head and focused on the road.

"You sure you didn't get even a little hard?"

"Well. Maybe a little. But that's only 'cause you were diddling yourself."

Mikey always knew the right answer to flatter a woman. He always spoke the truth, no matter the circumstance. Why couldn't more men be like her Mikey? Goddamn model male citizen if you asked her.

"Sure, sure. It's all the same to me," she said as she elbowed him playfully.

"It is?"

Leanna looked back out into the night sky. Soon they would be rich, and Teena would be dead. If she wasn't already. That was a night sky Leanna could get behind.

"Yeah, babe. It is now."

TWENTY-SIX...

Somewhere outside of Austin, Teena's pickup truck and horse trailer setup ambled down a long gravel driveway and up to the front door of a huge, sprawling ranch house. Beautifully gardened and maintained, the grounds were a sight to see for sure.

The entire drive there Teena tried to think of a reason, any reason, not to come here. To not pursue Leanna. She came up blank on both. Teena also couldn't come up with a single reason why she didn't come here sooner. Della had invited her enough times. There was always an excuse and it usually had to do with Leanna. Not this time. She was finally here because of Leanna, not in spite of her.

Della and Teena were part a tight-knit trio of Mama Francine's pupils for what felt like decades. Always reconnecting at just the right time. Learning and growing under their mentor. The third pupil, Mirabelle, fell out of favor with Mama a while back and Teena and Della stopped hearing from her soon after that. Mama wouldn't even mention her name going forward. Something about necromancy. Della tried to push for more information, but Teena convinced her to leave it alone. There was an ill feeling around Mirabelle's very name and Teena was content to let it be. Forever.

Once Mirabelle was gone, Della felt it the right time to pursue her affections for Teena. Advances Teena felt weird about but didn't rebuff entirely. Della could sense her apprehension soon after and ended it just as Teena was getting used to it all. Their reunions were few and far between after that. This visit was a good start in the mending fences department.

She popped out of the driver's seat and glided to the back of the horse trailer, humming softly. She fingered the pull-up hitch lock to the trailer's door as she gazed at her entourage inside.

"Just wait here, my lovelies. Mommy has some business to attend to."

"And what business would that be?"

Teena smiled without even looking for the voice.

"Old, unfinished business."

A sleek, well-dressed woman rounded the corner on Teena's truck and stopped, grinning at her, arms crossed. Tired eyes and smooth, soft skin. Long, wild cinnamon hair that ended at the small of her back. Della Suzanne still looked amazing. They were virtually the same age, but Teena felt herself dying inside and out with each passing year while Della Suzanne apparently had found the fountain of youth. And in Austin of all places.

"That old, huh?" Della raised an eyebrow. It brought Teena back to the good old days right away. She beamed and went to embrace Della tightly. They hugged for what seemed like ages. Teena didn't want it to end at all, really. Her friend smelled like spring flowers and the faintest hint of lime juice. It was wonderful.

"I had hoped you might be by some day," Della purred in her ear.

"And here I am."

"As it should be. What's in the trailer?"

"Just my horses. They'll be fine in there."

"Never liked the beasts. It's the eyes. They can stay in there for all I care."

127

Teena looked around at the breadth of Della's property with a grin. "Of course. Why would you ever have horses on a horse ranch?"

Della shook her head and chuckled. It was good to see her in her element. Teena would have been just fine if they remained outside and slept on the front doorstep. Anything to capture the moment and keep it a little longer.

"Well, come inside then, Tee-Tee," Della teased.

"You know I hate that name."

"And I love it. To pieces."

Della put an arm around Teena and walked her to the front door. The horse trailer rocked slightly, and a few sad, lonely groans emanated from it. The door to the trailer creaked open an inch or so as if someone had just quietly and covertly pulled up the lock and left it like that. *Quietly. Covertly.*

TWENTY-SEVEN...

D ad's Diner had seen better days but at least it wasn't the Cluck Shack. Ricky Richards couldn't figure out why these two knucklefucks had insisted on meeting him here. It was prime lunch hour, and the place was filled with a garden variety assortment of working stiffs trying to fill a hole in their gut before shuffling back to whatever slave wage job they were burdened with.

The things I do for you, Sharnell.

He was slouched in a booth that smelled like mildew-infused dishwater opposite two very odd-looking fellows. One was in his mid-thirties, stout and very hairy, with unkempt facial hair and a greasy trucker cap covering his ratty, sideburned coif. An oil-stained mechanic's work shirt with an embroidered name patch read *Lloyd Bob.*

The other fellow was very much on the tail end of his forties, tall and lanky. He wore a weird suit that looked like an undertaker's outfit from the Old West, complete with bolo tie and a five o'clock shadow. J.D. Tyson.

They looked like a vagrant, drunken version of Laurel and Hardy. Richards had a violently annoyed look on his face as he stared at them. Waiting for an answer.

"Think you can do that for me?"

"Shoot, the price is right and the target don't sound too difficult neither," Lloyd Bob said as he folded his arms.

"Hold on a second. What about the two gentlemen you mentioned? What are we walking into here?" Tyson was much more inquisitive than his partner. Richards appreciated it even though his patience was at its literal wit's end. He sighed and prepared to sink down to their level of intellect, as it were.

"Look, you came highly recommended by Sharnell. Fuck if I know why, but there it is. So this is your chance to get into the business. As long as you're packing and ready for anything, you can easily kill her and both of them smelly junkies lickety-split."

"That tranny done good by us in the joint. We owe 'im big time," Lloyd Bob said with pride in his voice.

"Don't... Don't use that word." Richards was one more shitty comment away from calling the whole thing off. These two couldn't find a whore in a whorehouse even if every whore was wearing a t-shirt that said *Hello! I'm a whore*. He made a mental note to never let Sharnell hear the end of this. Ever.

"What word? Joint?" Lloyd Bob was endearingly stupid; he'd give him that.

"Tranny. Disrespectful."

"Why? I seen them trannies all the time online. Tranny Trick, Tranny Trap, That Darn Tranny, Tranny Granny, you name it boss. Can't be that bad, know what I'm saying?"

"She's a bonafide lady and deserves to be treated like one."

"She got a pecker?"

"For the time being."

"Tranny don't seem so bad. What about shemale?"

"I think we're done here, gentleman. You have the details. You're either in or you're not. I gotta skedaddle. Like, yesterday."

Fucking uncultured idiots. He made a mental note to have Sharnell tell him the entire story of how she met these blobs of shit.

"Up front money is in order, Richard." Tyson knocked on the greasy diner table a few times. Richards surmised that probably meant Tyson thought he was being clever or classy or some such shit.

A silk ribbon on a pig, I wager. That's all it is.

Richards forcefully dug into his pocket and pulled out a wad of cash. He tossed it at Tyson.

"Five hundred each right now, another five each when the job is done."

"That was *not* the deal we struck, Richards."

"I'm a little strapped for cash right now. Your target's offspring, a sneaky little bitch of the highest order, has my payday in her pocket as we speak. All you got to do is kill that freaky old twat and report back to me. You'll both get paid like a motherfucker."

J.D. and Lloyd Bob consulted amongst themselves and whisper-mumbled a bunch of stuff at each other. Finally they broke the huddle and Lloyd Bob of all people was chosen to speak for both of them.

"So where this chick live at?"

TWENTY-EIGHT...

Leanna was now in the driver's seat as Mikey sawed logs passenger style. She flicked through the bunch of nothing channels on the radio but stopped cold when she saw a leviathan of a pink and purple neon billboard up ahead on the right. Lit up like a Dutch porn star's Christmas tree from 1983.

"FANNY'S HOT BOX"

"ADULT LOUNGE AND ESCORT PALACE"

"8 MILES UP AHEAD"

"AIN'T NO HOT BOX LIKE FANNY'S HOT BOX"

Holy. Shit.

This was it. A real field test. She felt like Einstein on the verge of one of his discoveries, whatever the fuck they were. She knew enough about it in a vague way and that was enough for her.

Leanna smacked Mikey hard mid-snore. "Wake up! Mikey! Look!"

Mikey woke with a start and moaned, rubbing the developing red handprint on his face. "Whaaaaat?"

"Fucking look! You're gonna miss it!"

Mikey spotted the massive billboard just as it was about to pass by. "Will ya look at that. Huh."

"I know, right?"

"We're goin' in, ain't we?"

"Mikey, we're not just going in. We're fucking *going in*."

"Don't we got some place to be? Is it a good idea to just stop—"

"Just say yes if ya love me."

Mikey sleepily nodded and gave her an acquiescing smile. It was all she needed for her to hoot and holler loud enough to fill a dozen Trans Ams. The car accelerated even more as it sped to its destination, which could now be seen off in the distance. A huge, neon monstrosity lighting up the dark, desolate desert. An oasis for fuckwits and freaks. For perverts and libido mongers. Leanna cackled as she saw the exit approach. A sex-charged red-carpet entrance rolled out just for her and Mikey.

It's perfect.

TWENTY-
NINE...

An orange El Camino covered in patchwork rust like a tangerine milking cow, headlights off, pulled up to Teena's house as silently as it could on a gravel driveway.

"Don't look like nobody's home," Lloyd Bob guessed.

"That could be what she wants, L.B." J.D. Tyson was one tiny step ahead of Lloyd Bob as usual.

~666~

The front door busted open with a violent smash. Flashlight beams penetrated the pitch-black house. No Leanna-style lockpicking here. So much for subtlety.

"It's my gut I tell ya, ain't no one here," Lloyd Bob insisted.

"Let us just see. Your gut is usually reserved for chili dogs and grape soda."

They searched the front room with fixed frowns. Teena's voodoo showcase did not amuse nor impress them one bit.

"Some weird ol' humdrum in here."

"Indeed. A practicer of the voodoo arts."

"A dang Negro witch if you ask me."

"Except she is Caucasian, brother Lloyd."

"Maybe on the outside."

They searched the bedroom. It looked like a normal fortysomething female-owned bedroom compared to that accursed front room.

"Nothin' freaky in here," Lloyd Bob said as he spat on the beige shag carpeting.

The kitchen held no secrets nor ambushes. Some dirty dishes strewn about, but nothing ominous.

"Nor here," J.D. Tyson whispered.

Back outside in the truth of night, J.D. and Lloyd Bob leaned against the El Camino with puzzled frowns.

"How we gonna find her if she's already skee-daddled?"

"How indeed."

"Just when ya could use a friendly neighbor o' sorts. Shoot."

"That's it."

"What's it?"

~666~

Zeb's ancient, ramshackle farmhouse was in dire need of repairs. It was even pitcher and blacker out there compared to Teena's place. The El Camino's headlights were the only whiff of illumination for miles. The engine was still running, and Lloyd Bob and J.D. were at the front door, knocking. Zeb answered after a few long moments.

"Well, what are two fellers like you doin' way out here? You wanna have some apricot cobbler and watch Luggage Wars with me?"

"Funny you should ask, feller. And yes to the cobbler." Lloyd Bob licked his lips as he pulled a gun from the back of his overalls.

THIRTY...

O n either side of a small yet roaring stone fireplace sat Teena and Della Suzanne in comfy armchairs, sipping tea from expensive china. The house was decorated in a weird combination of 19th-century English opulence crossed with Southwestern ranch deco. Queen Victoria meets Georgia O'Keefe.

"...But I have to confess, I was afraid you'd never visit. You know, people always say they'll come by as a nicety, but the reality is—"

"Don't peg me into that kind of category. You know why I haven't."

"Yes. But you can't let her run your life. She's had too many chances. More than anyone deserves."

"Mama Francine said basically the same thing. How often do you two talk?"

"It's what anyone with half a normal lick of common sense would say. She's actual poison to you now."

"I think I've just come to that realization recently, to be honest."

"And I haven't talked to Mama in years. Did she put you up to this? Wait...what did she say to you?"

A stiff chill pushed against Teena's flesh. She was certain Della and Mama were on speaking terms. Why wouldn't they be?

"Is there something you're not telling me? I thought—"

"Mirabelle visited me a few months ago."

That name. *The* name. It felt weird hearing someone else say it out loud. Away from the confines of her own head.

"We all agreed she was probably dead by now. You said yourself that—"

"She was here. In the flesh. Very much alive. And she had a lot to say about Mama."

I'm sure she did.

"Teena. You can't go back there. Not ever. It's not safe," Della continued.

"What? What do you mean not... Mama's the only person who's bothered to care about anything to do with me and my life, I'm not just going to—"

Teena saw Della's face fall just a bit, enough for her to pause mid-sentence. It put a firm little knot in her stomach.

"Oh, you know I didn't mean you. It's just... I have nowhere to go. I have nothing left. My stays over there are all I have to look forward to these days. That's literally it. Rather sad, I suppose."

"You came here. That's the first step. You don't have to leave."

The knot loosened into a handful of butterflies and Teena's face went all warm. She wanted to stay. So very bad. Forever.

But...

"I must see this through. I can't leave it alone. Not this time."

"What did she do this time?"

"She's used up all her chances with me. That's what she's done."

"And you're on a wild goose chase after her for what? To do what?"

Teena shifted her gaze away from Della. The shadows were creeping closer. She could feel them just outside the walls of the room. She stared at all the cattle skulls on the walls, trying not to think about the shadows. What was with these skulls? She never mentioned anything remotely resembling such a hobby back in Haiti.

"These are almost voodoo, in a way," Teena deadpanned as she changed the subject.

"Teena. You're not going to—"

Teena just sipped her tea. "This is delicious."

"Just because I said she's not worth saving doesn't mean she's—"

"We already tried jail. It didn't work."

"We?"

"I convinced Ronnie to turn her in. He had evidence of her drug dealing antics and a video of her anally violating a meter maid. She did eighteen months. She was supposed to do two years. Good behavior. Can you believe that? Only when she wants to."

"Teena. Where's Ronnie?"

"She got out almost three weeks earlier than that. God only knows who she seduced to get *that*. Three weeks. I was going to come home and get ready for her, make sure she didn't take anything. Maybe reason with her. She didn't tell anyone she was getting out that early."

Teena sipped some more tea, a slight tear escaping her eye.

"She went right to the house. She stole my love dust pouches. She—"

Teena inhaled sharply, almost dropping the teacup in her shaky hand.

"She strangled Ronnie to death. She just left him there."

"Teena you need to call the police. You can't do this alone."

"It's too late. She's done it to herself. It's—"

Teena broke down completely, sobbing heavily. Della looked stunned, but gently placed her teacup down and dropped to her knees, making her way to Teena, wrapping her arms around her tightly.

"It's okay, Tee-Tee. You're here. With me. I can't think of any other place you should be right now. You should have come sooner."

Teena reciprocated Della's touch, returning her own tight embrace.

"Thank you."

"Just... Just try not to think about her for one night. At least for tonight, okay? And promise me you won't go back to Mama's. There's more to tell you in the morning."

In the morning? I promise.

Teena knew deep down she couldn't keep that promise, try as she most likely would. Della loosened her hug and looked Teena directly in her face, oh so very up close. Right into her eyes. She brushed a lock of hair from Teena's vision and smiled sweetly. Teena smiled back just enough and kissed Della on the lips like a long-lost lover. *She is a long-lost lover.* Della kissed her back without hesitation. It felt like she was smiling as they kissed. The quiet passion between them rose as they reached for each other's shoulders, pulling down their tops. Teena saw Della's tattoo of Venus on her shoulder, exposed. It fascinated her to no end. When they were in Haiti, she caught herself staring at it all the time. It aroused her and the thought of it kept her company on those quiet, dark nights in her hut when it was just her. No Della. No Mirabelle. Just her and Venus.

Della let loose a small moan as Teena kissed Venus, almost trying to eat the patch of tattooed flesh. The feel of it was warm, alive, appreciative. It had been so long. She wondered why she didn't embrace Della wholeheartedly all those years ago. Leanna had taken up so much real estate in her head that seeing clearly was a veritable feat of strength for Teena. While she tried to push her daughter's infection of an existence from her mind, she gently guided Della down to the floor as the fire crackled and popped, seemingly bristling with excitement for the show it was about to witness.

"Are you sure this time? You..."

"—Shhh..."

No further words were uttered by Teena. She proceeded to kiss and lick and suck every inch of Della Suzanne's body, which flinched and shuddered every few long seconds at Teena's touch. Della soon found herself undressed and covered in Teena's gentle tongue trails. Teena came up for air after successfully stripping Della discreetly and drank it all in. She was beyond gorgeous bathed in the firelight, her skin seemed to shift and reach out for Teena, the woman's very cells wanting to fuck Teena so very badly. Teena unbuttoned her sleek black dress and let it fall to the ground, joining Della in the warm glow of achingly aroused nakedness.

"I knew you'd come around some day."

"I never needed to come around, my love. I was there the whole time. I just wasn't ready."

Della smiled and pulled Teena to her and at the same time brought her legs up and over Teena's shoulders, letting them rest there as Teena didn't miss a single beat and placed her head in between Della's thighs, kissing her clit a few times before getting right to it and using her tongue to show Della how much she wanted this. How much she had been thinking about this all these years. Perhaps knowing exactly what was on her lover's mind, Della quickly found a rhythm in Teena's strokes and dug in, pressing against her face and rocking her hips in a small circular motion.

"Oh. My. Godddddd...."

It wasn't long before Della reached the end of her journey and came with a soft bellow that ended in a jumbled dragging out of Teena's name in blunt appreciation.

Teena soon came up for air and they kissed again, this time hungrily, wildly, knowing that stealing shy looks or exchanging mild, flirty compliments were now a thing of the past.

Teena broke the seal on their mouths and held Della's face in her hands greedily.

"...My turn."

They both broke out into a grin as a coyote howled in the hills somewhere nearby. Della flipped over and took Teena down to the ground with nimble precision.

"Yes, Tee-Tee."

The shadows seemed to recede a little right then and there.

THIRTY-ONE...

Leanna and Mikey stood in front of the entrance to Fanny's Hot Box. Mikey scratched his head. Leanna's arms were folded and lips pursed. Both deep in thought. Allegedly.

The outside of the Hot Box was a garish hot pink and purple neon pussy fart. It seems to be a mixed sexuality establishment. Gay fellows, drag queens, hot chicks, college bros, trans men and women of all adult ages, and all other kinds of people milled about and freely flowed in and out, boisterous, and wild.

The massive pro-wrestler bouncer outside hadn't stopped staring at Leanna's breasts for at least a good five minutes. And he didn't seem happy about it for some reason.

"How much dust we got left?" Leanna asked Mikey.

"Uh... You gave that dirty shitbag Jiman two. We used up one whole one ourselves. Another to that law dog you scissored without asking me. Makes eight left. Surprised you didn't give one to that skeezy hitman."

"I don't trust him."

"Compared to everyone else you're planning on double-crossing?"

"*We're* double-crossing. And him especially. He'd be on our ass trying to steal our action if he knew what we're really doing this for." Leanna snapped her head toward the bouncer's direction and raised her voice a full octave. "You gettin' a good show, you fuckin' walkin' pituitary gland?"

The bouncer remained silent. Leanna lifted up her top, revealing her bare breasts to him. Pert yet not too perky. Leanna was proud of their natural, classical look. She often flashed men to remind them of their cosmetic inferiority compared to women like her. Women who had no problem taking what they wanted.

"Lee..."

"Look where you're at, baby," the bouncer replied, in the most monotone voice possible to human vocal cords.

There were plenty of females of all varieties with their breasts out, making merry like all get out. Leanna pulled her shirt back down, grimacing. Maybe taking what she wanted would have to wait for a moment. Her natural powers of perk were being drowned out by the boob circus taking place all around her.

Fuck.

She couldn't remember the last time she had to pay to get inside a club. It made her skin itch something fierce. "What's the cover?" Leanna asked the bouncer, gritting her teeth all the while.

"Hundred. Each."

"Fucking what?"

"Lee, just stay calm—"

Leanna pushed Mikey out of the way and got right up in the bouncer's face.

"How much?"

"Two hundred each. Plus a two-drink minimum, you classy lady, you."

Leanna pulled out her new knife, AKA Flavio's old knife, and put it right to his throat, standing on her tippy toes.

"Fucking *how* much?"

"For two South Texas shitheads like yourself, two hundred is a discount. Wanna try for three hundred?"

"Jesus Christ, Lee!"

Just then, a sassy, brassy middle-aged woman dressed like Madonna circa 1995 pushed her way through the in-and-out throng of partygoers and sidled up next to Leanna and the bouncer. Black and gold bustier, knee-high boots, and a whip holstered on her golden belt. Pale, well-maintained skin that smelled like orange peels. Thick, braided dark brown hair that came all the way down to the backs of her knees. Miss Fanny in the flesh.

"You can't demand a refund if you haven't even been in yet, sugar," she virtually growled at Leanna with a grin.

"Stuff your muff, granny. This is between me and Big John Studd here."

Miss Fanny pulled out a tiny .22 Magnum Sidewinder muff gun from her feathered codpiece and casually aimed it at Leanna, cocking it with unmistakable intent. Leanna remembered the cute little firearm from one of Mikey's over-animated gun talks. Most of it went in one ear and out the other, but the teeny Sidewinder stuck. And here it was. No one else around seemed to even give a shit that a firearm had just been brandished. Maybe this was Leanna's kind of place after all.

"Drop the knife and let's go have some fun, you sexy little sparkplug."

Leanna stared through the bouncer and his dull, bovine-like eyes, then back and forth between Mikey and Miss Fanny, muttering under her breath.

"Baby, put down the knife. Ain't worth getting shot over no how, no way."

"Listen to your hot-ass boy toy, here. He's got wisdom."

"Put down the knife before I sucker punch you straight to hell," the bouncer said.

"Don't mind Edgar. He's just fiercely loyal to a fault. Got a nice cock, too. Wanna see?"

Leanna grunted violently as she relented and put away her knife.

"Thank you, Miss Fanny," Edgar replied, still void of any discernible emotion. Positive *or* negative.

"Jesus, Lee."

"Come again with the how much?" Leanna asked.

"Fifty each, plus a round of free drinks. Sexy couple discount."

"That's more like it," Leanna said under her breath, incapable of saying thank you under any circumstance.

Miss Fanny extended her hand to Mikey.

"Miss Fanny, at your service."

Mikey hesitated a moment before kissing her hand awkwardly. Leanna cleared her throat at that.

"Let's see what kind of trouble we can get into tonight, what do you say?" Miss Fanny joined them arm in arm with a wink.

"Yeah, whatever grandma. Just show us to the bar." Leanna didn't trust this cabaret cunt as far as she could throw her and made a mental note to kill her before they left. And the fucking bouncer, too.

Edgar. What a stupid fucking name for a bouncer. Or Anyone for that matter.

Miss Fanny ushered them both inside through all the happy, drunken chaos.

Time for the real test, Teena. Wish you were here, bitch.

~666~

Leanna's mildly impressed opinion of the exterior to Miss Fanny's Hot Box was quickly grabbed by the scruff of its neck and thrown off a fucking cliff as soon as she saw the interior.

Jesus Fuckaduck H. Christ on a dildo-topped pogo stick.

As Miss Fanny led her and a slack-jawed Mikey through the floor-to-ceiling purple-carpeted lobby to the main lounge, all Leanna could think about was how much direct-action dick and collateral damage pussy she was going to get in this place. Sex was happening everywhere, with or without her. As casual as could fucking be. Futons and ottomans, divans and settees, all purples and pinks, and all filled to the brim with gyrating, thrusting, and undulating human beings. There wasn't a single person left out of the copulation loop from where Leanna could see. She wanted to join in right then and there. The love dust would blow this place apart like a powder keg of cum, sweat, and probably a little bit of blood.

Miss Fanny noticed the bladed cogs turning in Leanna's spiked steel trap of a mind.

"Not just yet, little miss. You haven't even seen the center ring of this circus yet, so keep your clothes on."

No sooner than Miss Fanny uttered those words, they crossed the threshold to the main lounge. A gigantic, gilded bird cage of an exhibition grounds. A huge stage dominated the center of each of the three walls Leanna could see from where they were standing. High up in the ceiling, clusters of built-in silver cages containing dancers and exhibitionists of all persuasions and disciplines entertained the masses from a safe distance. Each main stage featured a different show: one for burlesque, one for drag, and the other for traditional pole dancing and stripteases. The music was so loud in there that Leanna was certain she had already lost her hearing and this was the aftereffects of a bout of tinnitus from hell. Servers by the dozens brought food and drinks to and from the massive room, weaving in and out of the people. The *people*. Not an audience, per se, but clusters of slow-moving orgies. Occasionally taking a break for the odd drink or snack, the humans in these clusters were interested in mostly only one thing: vigorous, athletic, showman-like *fucking*.

Miss Fanny found them a sleek circular table and a few high-back chairs as a base camp and wasted no time looking Leanna up and down once more.

"Let's see what we're working with here, huh?"

Leanna didn't have to be told twice. She was in her element. Might as well show off her business cards. She quickly pulled off her top and let her breasts hang free. Mikey smiled earnestly at the sight. He knew what was up. Miss Fanny eyed them with what seemed like reverence. She took a few steps closer and got her face mere inches away from the girls. She nodded and rubbed her hands a little too vigorously.

"Ah. A nice, full B cup. Very lovely, my darling. I think it's time to introduce you to my party guests."

Right as she finished her declaration, a few naked and perspiring partygoers spotted Leanna and made their way over to her. Mikey intercepted one especially excited young man with zero body fat and a confident, unabating erection and punched him square in the stomach.

"Back off, you hear?" He was angry and turning redder by the second. This was definitely not his element. Probably just force of habit. Leanna appreciated the bizarre chivalry in such a place but also felt sorry for him. She was going to have get him seventeen different kinds of fucked up to enjoy this night – this place – even just a little bit.

"Easy, tiger. I think she wants to mingle. Apologize to the young man," Fanny said to Mikey as she rubbed his biceps attentively.

Mikey placed an awkward hand on the guy's shoulder as he stuttered a heartfelt apology. The guy's erection was still front and center.

This place is where the pro-fessionals come to play. God damn.

"It's alright, Mikey. Take a look around you. See how many people are looking at you with their fuck eyes?" Leanna said to Mikey, undressing all the while.

Miss Fanny moaned in agreement and locked on to Leanna's breasts with her mouth and tongue; licking and sucking on her nipples and around her areolas like a hermit in the desert who just discovered an oasis.

Well alright, then. Kinda nice.

"Go on, shoo! I'll find you later, kay?" Leanna excused Mikey from being her chaperone as Miss Fanny grabbed on to Leanna and threatened to devour her.

Hands and mouths from every which way enveloped Mikey. He didn't even check to see if it was his kind of action. It didn't really matter here.

"Okay," he mumbled with a sheepish grin as he let the throng of sex carry him away to another part of the fucking grounds.

As Miss Fanny finished moistening Leanna's entire torso with her saliva, Leanna pulled out one of the purple pouches from within her removed short shorts and held it up high with a wide grin. It was time.

Miss Fanny gawped at it with more than a little childlike wonder and asked, "What's that, my lovely Leanna?"

Oh, I got something for that ass, yessiree.

"Try some. It'll make your night. I guarantee it."

Miss Fanny cocked her head and smiled sideways.

"What are you up to, girl? Is it some kind of cocaine? Ecstasy? Tell me!"

"It's a Corpus Christi delicacy, Miss Fanny."

Leanna held the pouch close to her other hand, gently dumped out a small pile of it and gave Miss Fanny the "come hither" finger wag. The potent aroma of lilacs and copper filled their immediate area.

"That smell... What is it?"

"Just fucking try it, will ya?"

Fanny closed in on Leanna's hands and gave a stalwart sniff of the stuff. It was up her nose like a rubber hose in no time. She snapped her head back and after a short moment of confusion, her fingers did the walking right down to Cooch Town.

"Knock it off! Look around you, lady. Your empire awaits, know what I mean?"

Miss Fanny regained her composure and wherewithal long enough to realize what Leanna was on bout.

"Oh, Jesus Christ. Jesus fucking Christ. What is this stuff?"

"It's the key to the greatest night of your life. Grab a partner and do-si-fucking-do all night long."

They exchanged evil smiles and soon after, Fanny grabbed Leanna in a death grip of a tongue swap and threw her to the floor. Leanna wasn't used to not being the aggressor. A slight pinch of fear gave way to genuine excitement as a lover with way more experience was about to rock her fucking world. As Miss Fanny descended upon Leanna with cosmically lustful eyes, she wondered if Mikey was having a good time.

"Found my partner for the hoedown, or should I say ho down?" Miss Fanny moaned as her lips closed in on Leanna's breasts again.

~666~

The night oozed through the Hot Box and Leanna's very soul like an amorous nocturnal stalker, masked up and with all the right moves. Fingers, tongues, cocks, breasts, pussies, all of it combining to form a chimera of pleasurable touching and a cacophony of delighted orgasms. Nothing was off limits and not a single person said no once everyone was under the influence of the dust. Leanna made sure to ration it as minutely as possible so everyone could get a hit and still feel the full effects of her mother's creation. Leanna was sure at this stage of the game that she herself knew how to use the stuff, *wield the stuff*, much more skillfully than Teena probably ever did. If not, then why was it sitting stuck in some stupid fucking trunk in a living room of a house that nobody gave a shit about?

Miss Fanny was a wild and attentive lover. She made Leanna cum thirteen times as they traded off partners and came back to each other over the course of the night. Mikey returned to her a few hours after everything had started, a baker's dozen of the Hot Box's ladies of the night pawing and fawning over him, following her man everywhere he went and any time he moved. She gave him and his new friends a proper smattering of the dust without even saying a word to him. Well, it was a proper smattering for anyone but Leanna and Mikey. They required more than just a pinch compared to these rank first-timers. These love dust newbies. When they were sure no one was looking at them, they would each snort a little more and a little more until they were at the larger doses they had become accustomed to. Mikey linked up with Miss Fanny and choked her with one hand as he took her from behind. Leanna masturbated to his domination of the mistress of the house, making them watch as a few young gigolos and college boys sucked on Leanna's toes as they stroked themselves. It was a *very* good orgasm, if Leanna was being honest. Top twenty on the dust for sure.

More and more employees and guests of the Box caught wind of the eye-of-the-storm orgy that was forming on the main showroom's mezzanine and gravitated toward it with hungry eyes and noses. Leanna and Mikey had to constantly shift focus from whoever they were fucking (or being fucked by) to dole out the dust in proper amounts. Once everyone was on the dust, though, the full-on Roman Empire orgy that ensued was something that neither Leanna nor Mikey would have ever been able to even dream of in a million lifetimes. A dream of a dream of a dream half-remembered in idle moments where you're not sure if it was ever real or just your brain wanting it to be real.

Ronnie wouldn't even have been able to get it up without at least one damn horse or midget milling about. Sucks to be him, Leanna thought as Edgar the bouncer slid his cock into her as she lay sideways, tonguing a young server girl's asshole as the same girl blew Mikey like there wasn't a single other thing on the planet of any concern to her whatsoever.

Before long, the mezzanine was no longer enough space to contain the shifting, throbbing, undulating throng of pure fuck that spiraled out of any normal control and spilled down the stairs and into the showroom proper as well as out into the front lobby and bar area. No place was safe from the stain of pussy juice, man spunk, and creampie leftovers. Leanna found herself drifting away from her starting area and carried by the spasming masses down the stairs and into the virtually bottomless pit of sex in the main showroom. There was no escape, and after a few long gazes around her, she didn't want there to be an escape. This was all her doing. All her design. Music thrummed and pumped in her head. She let anyone and everyone touch her. Suck her. Lick her. Pleasure her. There was no way her mother could have ever foreseen how her creation could be used on this massive of a scale. Teena thought small and Leanna thought big and that was that, Leanna decided. How could it get any bigger than this? There was one thing pulling at the back of her mind, though. *Mikey.* She looked for him, reached out for him, searched for him in the mass of the dust-filled faithful. She *wanted* him. Not just in a sex way. She wanted to hold him, touch him, stay with him for the rest of the night. Was that the dust wearing off or getting stronger? Was she dying? She was finding it hard to breathe a little. Were those tears she was crying? For Mikey? Or for someone else?

...Teena?

As a thick, barrel-chested man in his fifties with a long, scraggly beard tied together with an elastic band and worn and stretched out U.S. Navy tattoos mounted her and began thrusting like a broken piston in an abandoned oil field, she pretended it was Mikey who was railing her. It made it more pleasurable. It even brought her close to completion. Maybe the dust really was wearing off? Or maybe she was losing her edge. She would have sworn on a stack of bibles she saw Mikey on the stairs, reaching out for her as well. It was hard to breathe. It was hard to see. It was too much all at once to take. Leanna's eyes drooped and her throat screamed for water. The last clear thought she had before she blacked out was what if her mother showed up here? Saw them all doing this? What if she saw Leanna pulling off what she never could? Would she cry? Would she laugh? Would she simply join in?

Dead people don't join in on orgies, you dumb bitch...

THIRTY-TWO...

Leanna and Mikey's accidental crime scene was taped off to a comical degree; police swarmed all over the place, combing for evidence. Ricky Richards stood off to the side surveying the situation with a tired frown. He waved over a very young-looking cop he recognized, Officer Dwight Strickland. Wet eyes, acne-ridden face. Small hands. The puppy pig shuffled over with a roll of his eyes.

"Evening, Dwight."

"Richards, what the frig are you doing here? Corpus Christi's a long way's away."

"I'd say the same about you. Left the good ol' Body o' Christ for the bright lights of Fort Stockton, huh?"

"What do you want, merc?"

Richards handed Strickland a folded hundred.

"I'm on assignment."

Strickland took it while looking around for prying eyes.

"Fine. What do you wanna know? But you gotta make it quick, okay"

"As luck would have it, I'm tracking a particularly annoying couple of lunkheads. They owe me oodles of money and one of them's skipped parole, like a good degenerate."

"Think they did this?"

"Maybe. Dunno. Can't say for sure. Wouldn't put it past them. How long you been here?"

"Uh, less than an hour. Got a call from the store owner; said he heard two gunshots about fifteen, twenty seconds apart. Came around and saw two bodies like the ones right over yonder. Turns out they're career thugs. Car jackings, ATM holdups, tag team sexual assaults; mostly on men if you believe it. Looks like a robbery gone the worst kind of wrong, you ask me."

"I didn't. And thanks. You know, there's always room for another young lion in my stable if you get tired of the swine farm."

"I'm flattered."

Richards turned to leave. Almost.

"Say, kid. You wouldn't know if there's anything unusual on the highway up ahead. Anything out of the ordinary at all past tourist traps and shitty burger joints. Would you?"

An older cop with a perpetually angry face back at the crime scene proper spotted Strickland talking to Richards and it looked as if his head would explode from such a transgression.

"Strickland! Get your twink ass back to work!"

"Coming!" Strickland thought hard for barely a second, the stress of being spotted too much for him. "Shoot, I don't know. I gotta go."

Strickland jogged a couple of steps, stopped, faced Richards again with a panicked look of clarity. Richards was already heading back to his car, singing a David Allan Coe song to himself.

"Hey, I think there's a big ol' whorehouse a couple hours up the road. Freddy's Love Shack or something. Can't miss it. Other than that, ain't nothing else out here."

Richards squinted weirdly and smiled sideways without looking back at Strickland.

It can't be this easy. It just can't.

"Thanks, twink."

~666~

About an hour down the road, Ricky found one of his old haunts still alive and well. The Slim Mickey, a bar for expats of the law of all types. Rogue bounty hunters, corrupt bail bondsmen, disgraced cops, mobsters on the squeal, and sometimes even international mercenaries and arms dealers (when they happened to be in town). It was a slow, smoky little joint just off I-10. It used to be all by its lonesome save for a flophouse motel a few hundred yards back, but in the 90s a Steak & Ale and a 7-Eleven popped up next to it and both managed to survive to present day on life support and grift money.

Richards practically rolled out of his car, as his legs and butt were asleep from so much driving lately, and chuckled at the very sight of the place. He put his hands on his hips and adjusted his belt, more out of habit than necessity.

"Hello, darlin'. You miss me? I sure missed you."

The parking lot was nearly full. Tonight must be special. He knew he'd get at least a morsel of intel about what lay in wait just up the road at whatever lust trap Strickland alluded to. Chadwick's Butt Hut? Something like that. Despite his reputation, Richards was not a fan of brothels and whorehouses pers se. Strip joints? Sure. Those were fine. But paying for intercourse? It wasn't that hard to get laid for Richards and he also enjoyed being in committed relationships. That came to the surprise of most people who crossed his path. Bounty targets, assassin partners, old mob acquaintances - they all tried to get him to wet his dick away from his steady missus, whoever that may have been at the time. It was no can do according to Ricky. He was, for the most part, a one woman man and took pride in remaining that way. His ex-wife, Kimberly, was his best friend for a long spell. Until he met Sharnell at an all-nighter poker game at his friend Runaround Rob's place. It was love at first sight. They all warned him she was a different kind of lady but he didn't care. Love was love and he made a lot of adjustments to make room in his heart for Sharnell. It wasn't like he was going to march up and down the street draped in a special flag every year in a parade or anything but he sure did get wise to a lot of things he had been ignorant about before. Though he tried to make it work with his wife as best he could, when she found a new kind of porn on his laptop and rebuffed his attempts to get her to fuck him with a strap-on (to "spice things up" in the bedroom) the writing was blatantly on the wall. She departed in a cloud of quiet without a Dear John letter in sight. She even left most of her things. Probably just enough to fit in a suitcase went with her. They hadn't any (nor wanted any) kids, so the separation ended up pretty clean. If you call never hearing from your wife ever again "clean". Richards joked to anyone who would listen she became a nun to counter his dirty life and times. Inside, though, her departure stung like the dickens. Sharnell soon made most of the pain go away. She was strong, funny, and a next-level lover. Giving, thoughtful, and fiercely loyal. The hurt of Kimberly leaving him smoothed out over time but on a few random late nights here and there, Richards would get to missing her painfully bad. That's when a just purchased case of Miller or

Yuengling would disappear in a night and Sharnell would have to give him some space. And she did. She was such a good woman. Ricky didn't deserve her. He tried like hell to live up to deserving her, though. And this right here was abso-fucking-lutely part of living up to it.

Ricky steadied himself and shuffled to the front door. Revolver firmly tucked in the back of his jeans, covered by his leather jacket. He lit a smoke with his Zippo and prepared to enter the lion's den of ornery, cantankerous, and downright bloodthirsty perpetrators of all kinds of unsavory anti-law actions.

He could hear the jukebox spitting some Leonard Cohen from outside. Sounded like something from Cohen's *The Future* album. Could it be "Democracy"? *No, couldn't be that on-the-nose on a night like this.*

Richards thought about Leanna again and her stupid-ass man-boy of a squeeze. They'd most definitely be having their fun at that place up the road tonight. He'd let them. It'd be the last lick of true pleasure they were gonna have on this planet. When he and Sharnell got to them and got to the bottom of what they were really up to out here, fun would be the last goddamn thing on the menu. And that was the god's honest as far as Ricky Richards was concerned.

As he pulled open the front door and ambled inside, "Democracy" by Leonard Cohen played loud and smooth from that old reliable jukebox in the far corner of the place, right next to the cigs machine and the hallway leading to the pissers.

Nose on the nose on the nose. Never change, Slim Mickey. Never change.

Ricky scanned the place. Everything was old and made of wood that also smelled old. Smoke of all kinds slathered the place in suspiciousness. Glasses clinked, cards were drawn and played, and women were tossed around from table to table until an interested party chose them to sit and stay a while.

He noticed a few old louts in the sea of new faces and harrumphed. Figures. Most of the old pros and legends had most likely "moved on" in some such way or another. It *had* been at least six or seven years since he'd been around here in any major way. At least the bartender was still the same round these parts. Richards grinned before whistling sharply the bartender's way.

Coots McMichael, the booze jockey in question, snapped his head Ricky's way and stared at him intently before letting a small smile escape his rankled mouth. The guy was tall, at least six-foot-six, and sported a ginger chinstrap of a sideburns-and-goatee apparatus.

"Coots! You silly old bastard! Gimme a Mickey's!" Richard shouted across the way. A few dudes looked toward the noise. Some had blank stares. Others recognized him and shook their heads in disappointment or rolled their eyes in annoyance before going back to whatever they were doing. No record scratch with the song stopping or anything like that here. Leonard Cohen played on as Richards licked his lips in anticipation of the cold brew that was about to come his parched way.

"I was wondering when I'd see your rat face around here again, bounty hunter."

"Private eye, now. Of a sorts, that is."

"So just a shitty hitman? Gotcha."

"Aw hell now, that any way to talk to an old friend? Don't matter how many years pass, I still saved your ass in Cheyenne. Never even asked for a favor."

"And you'll never let me forget that. I gotcha. So let me guess..."

Coots slid a Mickey's with the top popped off down the bar to Richards just in time for him to make it there and snatch it up. *Perfect timing. Guy's still got it, I'll be damned.*

"—You're here for the favor now. Yes?"

"It's a just an itty bitty one. Promise."

"Out with it. I already have a headache on account of your voice."

"I appreciate the flirt session but I'm just here for info. You know anything about that sex castle just up the way a piece? What's it called? The Hump Shack or some shit?"

Coots leaned in toward Richards considerably and lowered his voice more than a skosh.

"You mean Fanny's Hot Box? What the hell would you want anything to do with that place?"

"You know it?"

"Couple of the regulars here have checked it out. It's all fun and games on the outside but that place is trouble in a tuxedo times ten, Richards. Steer clear of it. I hope you don't have business there. If so, you're better off finding another line of work."

"That bad, huh? What could be so dangerous about a jizz joint?"

"The bird that runs it, she's fucked in the head. Like she thinks she's the Capone of the cunt trade. Nobody messes with Fanny Albright. Even the hombres that frequent this particular establishment, when they go to that place, they're on their best behavior. You tiptoe out of line at the Box, all kinds of impolite things can happen to you. Trust me. It's a den of fuckery at its rotten core."

Richards harrumphed to himself and downed the rest of his Mickey's.

"Another?"

Coots went and grabbed another Mickey's, popped the top and sent it sailing towards Ricky's waiting hand. He returned to Ricky's personal space and frowned.

"Last one and you gotta leave. Spivey's spotted you and he ain't alone tonight. You should leave."

Fucking Spivey. Of all the shitkickers to run into here.

Dale Spivey was one of the old regulars at the Slim Mickey who never ever got along with Richards. Their bar fight about fifteen years back sent three people to the ICU and two to the morgue. Plus plenty of other various injuries of the medical bill variety. Spivey was an ex-cop turned mercenary, which was just a fancy way of avoiding the term *hitman*. He was a surly, testy scumbag of the highest order and the older he got, the more violent he became.

"One for the road and I'm gone, old friend. Thanks for the info."

Coots was visibly annoyed but slid another cold, stubby bottle of Mickey's malt liquor ale Richards' way and made a shooing motion with his hands at him. Message sent loud and clear. As Richards downed his second bottle and took the third one for the drive, a stony and acidic voice interrupted the next song, Cohen's "Everybody Knows". *Must be Canadian night up in here.*

"Ricky mother-goddamn-fucking Richards. Will wonders never cease to be pieces of useless dogshit."

The short and stocky Spivey was only a few feet away from Richards, approaching at his side. Ricky felt trapped, like this was a prelude to an ambush. Sure enough, three younger men, probably lost in their mid-thirties somewhere, joined Spivey in surrounding Richards.

"Spivey in the flesh. How's tricks? I see you got yourself a new harem. You boys read about ancient Greek and Roman male mentorship? I guarantee Spivey here has."

"Real fucking funny, Richards. You still owe me for the Topeka job and you got the nerve to walk in here after all these years and not even acknowledge me?"

"Well, Spivey, I didn't check the handicap stall for a buttfucking four-way going on, so I'm sorry I didn't see ya right away."

Spivey pursed a sideways smile betwixt his lips and rocked back and forth on his heels.

"This here's Craig, Fitzy, and Boozler. They're my new hires. Consider what we're about to do to you a sort of on-the-job-training exercise. If you ain't gonna pay me back for Topeka outta your wallet, you're gonna do it outta your hide. Boys!"

Craig, Fitzy, and Boozler closed in on Richards and all drew switchblades in unison. It would have been impressive if Richards was part of the tabled audience taking the impromptu show in. Instead, he was the star of said show and it was just about showtime.

"Now boys, I know ya gotta impress yer boss and all that jazz but do you really wanna make a mess in here? Coots here don't really wanna clean up a bunch of bodily fluids tonight. You wouldn't make him have to do all that now would ya?"

"Don't worry, Ratface Richards, we'll clean up your blood and guts once we're done with you. Deal?" Spivey said as he rubbed his hands together.

And then they were on him, stabbing and slicing at him with lethal intent. All three of Spivey's pupils had deadly intent in their eyes and talking was useless at this point. So Richards pulled out his revolver and shot Craig in the face. A cascading bouquet of blood, brains, and skull erupted from the back of Craig's head after the bullet blasted through the guy's left eye. Dead Craig dropped his knife as his lifeless heap of humanity fell to the ground and the blade lodged in Fitzy's shoe.

As Fitzy screamed in pain and panic, a good number of the bar's seedy patrons moved their chairs and tables backwards to the other side of the room. They wanted to watch still, sure, but also wanted to keep a reasonably safe distance. Some of them started taking bets on who would survive. Others picked their favorites and started cheering for them.

With such a captive audience, Richards nimbly dislodged the blade from Fitzy's foot and stabbed him in the throat with it. Fitzy grabbed at his throat and with his arms occupied, Richards mule kicked the wannabe killer into the crowd and shot him in the chest, center mass. *Two down.*

Boozler, the biggest of the three, swung a right hand hard and fast at Richards and connected with his face. It threatened to put Richards' light out but he narrowly avoided such a turn of events as he shook the cobwebs out, smacked himself in the face and tackled Boozler's legs, bringing the fella down to the floor, where his size was less of a clear advantage.

"Take this prick out, Boozler! Look what he did to Craig and Fitzy! Break his fucking neck! You ain't worth shit if you—"

CRACK-A-BLAM!

In mid tirade, a shotgun blast to Spivey's back exploded his spine into plain view and shut him up for good, sending him to the dingy wooden floor in a bloody pile of shitty, past-his-prime, old man wreckage. Spivey fell pretty close to Richards and he could smell the old man's blood mixed with English Leather aftershave. Richards wasn't even sure they sold that shit anymore. *Must be a really fucking old bottle.*

Both Richards and Boozler ceased their struggle and looked up to see what the hell just happened. Or *who* the hell just happened.

Sharnell cocked her shotgun and ejected the round that slew Dirty Dale Spivey. She looked down at Richards and Boozler with an expressionless face.

"Are you done fucking around on the ground?"

"You made a rhyme, baby."

Sharnell fought a smile that spread fast and involuntarily.

"Get up for fuck's sake."

She trained her shotgun on Boozler and scowled.

"Back the fuck up and go get a drink or something. Fight's over, little man."

Boozler rose with his hands in the air and stammered a reply. "Spivey's pay wasn't that good. Can I buy you two a beer?"

Richards glanced over at his broken bottle of Mickey's he was looking forward to drinking on the way to Fanny's Hot Box.

"I'll take a Mickey's."

~666~

Back outside, in the clear light of night, Ricky nursed his bruised face with his new and super cold Mickey's. Sharnell was drink-less but smoked a cigar like she was the one who invented cigars.

"You sure you okay?"

"Yeah. I'll live. Thanks, baby."

Richards kissed Sharnell on the cheek and caressed her face.

"What are you doing, though? You gotta get your sexy behind to Tucson before any of the rest of us do."

"You're not going to that whorehouse. You can't."

"You don't gotta worry about me. That bitch is up to something else and I can smell the real money just out of reach. There's no way this was just a simple "kill my mom and skip town" deal. She's hiding the real score and I gotta see what it is. You just make sure you're at Drakesworth's before any of us like we planned. Pedal to the metal, speed your ass there, bribe any cops that get in your way, put 'em in your trunk, whatever you gotta do to get there first. You dig?"

Sharnell nodded with conviction and kissed her man right back.

"I dig. Be careful in that place."

"That's my girl. Thanks for checking in. Now if you don't mind, I got a date with an ever lovin' den of sin."

THIRTY-
THREE...

Teena dreamt of Ronnie. How could she not? His strangled face was imprinted on her brain. Probably forever.

She and Ronnie were at her dinner table, a meal just finished moments ago. They shared a joint and a bottle of wine. Cab Sauv. Ronnie's favorite. It became her favorite, too. Both sat solemn as they maintained an odd silence.

Until Ronnie broke it with a nervous voice.

"I just... I don't know if I can do this."

"You said yourself she's dangerous. Unpredictable. This is what she needs to learn her lesson."

"What if it doesn't? What if it just pisses her off even more? She scares the shit out me."

"We'll cross that bridge when we come to it. This needs to be done."

"The things she says. It's like she doesn't even realize how screwed up she is."

Ronnie grew more and more upset the longer they talked about Leanna. Like she haunted the very house they were in and merely mentioning her might summon her specter. Teena remembered being spooked herself at the combination of the eerie quiet in the house and his rising agitation.

"Then do something about it. You have the video. You have witnesses to corroborate your own experiences."

He didn't answer her. He just stared at the table, a lost little boy overtaken by a wave of adult responsibility. Teena grabbed his hands delicately, lovingly. Desperately.

"Do you love me?"

Ronnie nodded, still a child adrift.

"Do you trust me?"

"Yeah. I do."

"Then we need to do this. Together."

He nodded again and Teena reached in to kiss him. After a few seconds, he kissed her back.

That hesitation to kiss her in return bothered Teena then and it still did today. But now it also made her feel something else.

Guilt.

THIRTY-
FOUR...

Teena and Della Suzanne were entwined together underneath the silk sheets of a massive king-sized bed in total darkness. A mournful wail came from outside nearby. Neither one stirred from it yet. Another sad groan joined the first one. They echoed creepily in the very near distance. Della woke with wide eyes. She tried to gently rouse Teena.

"Teena..."

The two moans grew louder.

"Teena!"

Teena woke, groggy.

"What..?"

The groans rang out again. A croaking, creaking duet of sorrowful longing.

"There it is again!"

Teena knew the sounds well.

"Go back to sleep. It's okay."

"Okay? What in God's name is that?"

Teena didn't answer, instead cuddling up to Della, eyes still closed. The sounds got louder. Almost unbearable. And profoundly sad. Teena started humming that old creepy tune, soft yet firm this time.

Della realized something with an open mouth and wide eyes.

"Teena. Teena, where's Ronnie?"

"Outside. With Wallis. They're fine. Go back to sleep."

"What? When were you going to tell me this?"

"I just did."

Teena tried to kiss Della, to soften the blow, but she flinched backwards. The wide-eyed look of horror still there, not planning on leaving her face anytime soon, it seemed.

"You. You've... You've seen Mirabelle..."

Before Teena could even attempt to lie to her lover, the door to the bedroom burst open with a deafening CRRRACK. J.D. Tyson, armed with two .45 handguns and Lloyd Bob, armed with a sawed-off shotgun stormed in and aimed their weapons right at the rising commotion coming from the bed.

"What is this? You get out of my house! Now!"

"Della, I promise, I haven't seen her... I..."

Teena tried to put an arm around Della. To comfort her, to shield her. Something. Della batted it away angrily and tried to get up out of bed. Teena grabbed her and pleaded with her once more, ignoring the most recent and direct threat in the room with them.

"We kill this other broad?" Lloyd Bob asked his partner without breaking line of sight with the outrage of stark lesbianism right in front of his eyes.

"Do you even need to ask?" J.D. almost whispered back.

"Get down!" Teena tried, though it was too late at that point.

Lloyd Bob slayed a bewildered Della with a shotgun blast right to the chest. Her piercing scream rang out hard with the unmistakable grief of soul-tearing betrayal to Teena's guilty ears. Ribs and breastbone exploded with an invisible-to-the-eye punch of buckshot - a gout of red splattering onto Teena's face. She could see part of Della's heart through her chest as it beat its last. The look of shock and horror at the realization her returned lover was a necromancer like Mirabelle forever locked in place. Teena knew that face would stay right there in her mind alongside Ronnie's for as long as she lived. And right then that seemed to be only minutes more at best.

Teena's mind caught up with reality and she screamed a painful, throat-injuring scream while she held on to Della's destroyed, bloody body.

"She was mighty easy to find."

"Agreed. On account of her friendly neighbor, I would add."

Through her tears, Teena mounted a modicum of defiance.

"Oh, Zeb... You mindless animals will pay for—"

"Shut that voodoo skank mouth o' yers, ya old bag. Take yer killin' like a man."

"Worry not, the old fellow is still alive. Sucking consumables through a straw, most likely. But more alive than you will be in about five sec—"

Just then, Wallis and Ronnie crashed through the window next to the bed and grabbed on to Lloyd Bob and J.D., respectively, putting them into painful, messy headlocks. Their black spittle splashing and oozing onto the hitmen's dirty, scruffy necks.

"What in the f—"

"It is the undead, come to punish us for our sins!"

"God dang it all. Shoot 'em in the head!"

Lloyd Bob and J.D. tried in vain to aim for Wallis and Ronnie's noggins and ended up shooting everything else in the room but them. Teena had ducked for cover on the other side of a tall bureau, pulling and pawing wildly at Della's body to bring it down to the floor and protect it from further destruction. Her corpse landed with a squish and a dull thud as Teena slid all the way back against the wall, screaming into the deafening void of gunfire and growls.

J.D. and Lloyd Bob put up a valiant, if frantic, struggle but Wallis and Ronnie eventually broke every crunch-worthy bone in the screaming, grunting bodies of the two bargain bin assassins. Blood gushed from bite wounds, and bones perforated tattooed skin as Wallis and Ronnie chewed on J.D. and Lloyd Bob greedily. Teeth snapping bone, slurping marrow. Flesh pared like warm spare rib meat against hard, dead fingernails. The hitmen went from screaming to crying to nothing but automatic gurgles and hisses in what seemed like less than a minute.

Teena held her nose, the smell of one of them shitting themselves reaching her area of cover. One of Lloyd Bob's plumpy arms flew her way and smacked against the wall next to her, leaving a circular smash of bloody goo. Ronnie cackled at her, revealing himself to be the culprit.

Teena wiped tears from her flushed face and tried to push a polite response from her shaking mouth.

"I'm quite full but thank you so much, my sweetheart."

~666~

Wake up, Della. It's over now.

Hours later, the bedroom looked like a Lizzie Borden diorama. Pulped and masticated body parts everywhere. Teena was even more beside herself, sobbing and clutching Della's shotgunned corpse. Wallis and Ronnie stiffly rose and shuffled over to their distraught mistress, wailing and moaning right along with her. A hideous cacophony of sorrow.

Teena had a fleeting thought of bringing Della back like Ronnie and Wallis and it made her hate herself. She wanted to die right there. Close the circle for good. She grabbed a hold of Wallis and clutched him in a grip of desperation. They had to go on. Leanna was responsible for all of this. But she couldn't leave Della like this. She couldn't.

Could she?

Wake up. Please.

THIRTY-FIVE...

The main bar and lounge of the huge whorehouse was slathered in somnolent nudity. The place looked like a South Beach gay bar crossed with Scarface's foyer. You couldn't see the floor at all. Hungover, writhing, snoring, groaning bodies as far as the eye could see. Hookers, customers, bouncers, college party hounds, Miss Fanny. You name it.

Mikey and Leanna were in the center of the whole mass of sex. Passed out, sweaty and completely in the buff. People were slowly coming to one at a time. Mikey stirred a bit, letting out a low, exhausted groan. He had a death grip on an expensive bottle of champagne and as he woke, he took a big swig.

"...Lee?"

Leanna was a few feet away and sandwiched in between a cherubic male exotic dancer and an incredibly attractive female hooker with excessively large and very fake boobs. And lots of wonderfully nasty tattoos.

What the fuck...

Leanna's head throbbed. From the booze. From the dust. And from whatever else they probably took last night. It was the worst hangover she'd ever been forced to endure. A jackhammer inside a mylar balloon.

Mikey saw Leanna stir and inch her way out of the sex sandwich she was stuck inside. She sported a fire engine red strap-on dildo.

"Lee!"

Leanna finally opened her eyes all the way and fixed them on Mikey. The bright light of day was a poison-tipped dagger to her eyes.

"Fuuuuuck..." Leanna shouted in a hoarse, dried out voice.

"Lee!"

"Hey."

Mikey pointed to the strap-on with bug eyes and gritted teeth.

"Oh. This? You don't remember?" Leanna remembered that part. After she came to from her blackout episode, Mikey's turn at bat awoke something inside him and Leanna wasn't one to shy away from helping others live their truth.

"What do you mean, Lee? Remember what?"

"You were fucking Miss Fanny and insisted I drill you with a strap-on 'til you passed out."

"No I didn't—"

"So I did."

"What?!"

"And that was after you had your violent-ass way with about a dozen other people. You musta been blacked out or something. It happens sometimes on this shit."

"Lee..."

"Everyone who even looked at you got a good fuckin'. I have to admit, I was a little intimidated."

Mikey looked like he was about to vomit. The blood ran from his face, leaving a pale visage of regret and grim realization. He really needed to accept his predilections and cease with all the repression. Men and their hang-ups. Leanna had the mind to dress Mikey down about it if she didn't have the *Hangover From Planet X* drilling a hole into her frontal lobe right then.

175

Mikey looked around in awe at the mass of human sex surrounding them. "Jesus. How many bags did we—"

"*Six*. We had the goddamn place feening, babe. Greatest night ever. Miss Fanny killed two people while you were fucking her—"

"That's enough. We gotta get out of here, Lee. Where's the rest of the dust?"

"Shhh! Shut up with that shit. Had to knife a guy who tried to swipe the rest of it. Once everything got crazy, everyone pretty much forgot about it. They were all having the time of their shitty lives. Now that everyone's sober—"

"Christ, Lee. We need to leave. Right n—"

A shotgun cocked louder than an atomic bomb in such quietude. A gloriously naked Miss Fanny had said shotgun pointed right at Leanna. Her breasts were breathtaking in the morning. Leanna still couldn't decide if they were real or fake and that alone was worthy of a story on a day that wasn't today.

"Looks like we got ourselves some early risers," Miss Fanny chortled.

From all around the huge room, scores of naked hookers popped up, armed with all kinds of guns and knives.

Fucking crafty harlots. Leanna was impressed. This felt like one out of her own playbook. But she had to get Mikey out of here in one piece. No time for grandstanding.

"You bring us manna from heaven and think you can just stroll out of here like nothing happened? Like we didn't commune with the gods all night long? You can't just shut that off, my little peach pie."

Miss Fanny snapped her fingers so hard it made her tits wiggle.

"...Edgar!"

From the throng of crusty nakedness rose Edgar the bouncer, about a dozen feet away from Mikey and Leanna. Void of clothes and apparently a hangover as well. Impressive, Leanna mused. Especially after last night. She remembered him being hung but not *this* hung. His dick looked like an adult elephant's trunk if it were Frankensteined onto a mannequin from a big and tall store. It was almost laughable if their situation wasn't so dire.

But Leanna laughed anyways.

"I can't believe I took that thing inside me. Jesus Christ. Did you call the fire department and let them know you still have their high pressure riot hose?" Leanna said with a guffaw as she put her hands on her hips.

"Lee, now's not the time for funnin'. I got a really bad feeling about this."

"That's probably the Grey Goose mixing with the dust. Drink some water and you'll be fine, babe."

"Shush, harlot. In order to have the honor of being my bitch boy bootlicker, you have to fight Edgar here to the death. Fifteen fights over five years and my sweet boy here has never lost."

"But... I don't wanna fight him. And I don't wanna be lickin' your boots neither, ma'am. I thought we had a good time last night. Didn't we?" Mikey asked with an embarrassing level of earnestness.

"I didn't ask you for your opinion on anything, you dimwitted cum jockey. You're not leaving here in any way shape or form. What don't you get? You may use whatever you can find lying around to defeat your opponent. The only rule is to kill or be killed. Now, *fight*!"

"Yes, Miss Fanny," Edgar responded, totally monotone. As if he were a zombie himself. Teena would probably love this dude.

Mikey flinched and looked around for something, anything. Edgar was fast approaching at a steady lumber - he'd be on Mikey within a few good Mississippis. Leanna scanned the area for an assist. Nothing but dildos and liquor bottles as far as the eye could see.

When in Rome, yeah?

Leanna snatched the strap-on attached to her waist and unfastened it with the quickness. "Catch!" She tossed it to Mikey and then immediately bent down to procure an empty champagne bottle near her feet. "And this, too!"

As Mikey had both makeshift weapons in hand, Edgar was a foot away. Mikey swung away with the heavy rubber dildo as hard as humanly possible and all it did was bounce off of Edgar's muscular cheekbones.

"Fuuuuck... Lee, get back..."

Mikey swung option B and before the champagne bottle could even reach Edgar's noggin, the bouncer grabbed Mikey's wrist, shook the bottle out of Mikey's hand through sheer force, and watched as it dropped to the ground and shattered. Mostly the bottom half. The neck part remained intact with a jagged, jangly ending to it.

The headbutt came next. It rang Mikey's bell, bloodied his nose, and sent him to the floor in a thudding, squeaking heap. Flesh pushing against tile made for a sickening sound, Leanna decided.

"Get back up, Mikey! You can't kill 'em on the fuckin' floor!"

Mikey threw an exasperated glare her way and tried to scramble to his feet. Edgar was back on him again and laid in a solid right fist to Mikey's face, flattening him once more.

The sea of armed hookers had formed into a ragged circle of onlookers of varying barrier thickness all around. Guns and eyes both trained on the clothes-less smackdown currently happening. Miss

Fanny stood on top of the bar, lording over everything with a confident grin.

"That's it, Edgar! Pound that twink's face into the ground! If you ever want to felch with your mistress again you'll kill him in the next thirty seconds!"

Jesus fuck, that's foul. Even Leanna of all people wasn't much into felching. That was saying something for sure. Swapping cum with those two nutjobs? It almost brought her to a solid vomit. But that would distract Mikey and cause him to vomit as well. *Focus, Lee, focus...*

"Kick his ass, Mikey! You want me to tell 'em what you did at that truck stop, you nasty fucking ho?"

That seemed to do it. Mikey's face went a deep red almost instantly, aside from the blood already accrued there mere seconds ago. He clambered to his feet and dodged a front kick from Edgar, regaining his footing and assuming proper fighting stance. Mikey did train a little in Brazilian jiu jitsu at the old fight gym in Corpus Christi but had to quit after he broke another guy's leg in a sparring session. Well, more like fractured the guy's leg in two places. He was bragging about how he was going to fuck Leanna while Mikey watched which did not sit too well with Mikey (to completely undersell his reaction). Leanna had never seen Mikey so aggressive and wild. Needless to say, she came hard in her jean shorts as soon as bone had broken skin.

Right about then, in that frantic Hot Box moment, Mikey was approaching *that* level of aggression. Anti-cuck aggression times infinity. Leanna clapped her hands and shook her ass at Mikey.

"Kill him and take me from behind, baby! I'll even pretend to be your stepmom this time!"

Mikey had had a huge crush on Maye Freeman, his dad's last wife before the old man came out as gay about five years ago. Leanna was the only one Mikey had told his secret to and she rewarded him by stealing some of Maye's clothes and dressing up as her during one particularly hot lovemaking session. Mikey tried to make it last as long as possible but once Leanna started acting and sounding like Maye as they fucked, all bets were off. It felt like a Gatling gun had went off inside her. Since then, Mikey had been obedient to Leanna no matter what. Teena couldn't sway him and none of the local skanks could even get some fool-around time with him anymore. And when Maye Freeman herself finally came around and tried to seduce Mikey, he turned her down flat. That one surprised the shit out of Leanna. He was *hers*, no doubt about it. When Leanna dated Ronnie for a spell right before her stint in prison, he remained faithful to her when he didn't even have to be at all. That one time was the only time Leanna offered to roleplay as Maye. The look on Mikey's face when Leanna uttered the word 'stepmom' just now was something Leanna wished she could have photographed and commissioned into a high faluting painting that would hang in the fanciest of museums. Maybe that Loov place in France.

Mikey threw two wicked hard jabs to Edgar's midsection - both a left and a right. That would have removed the wind from the sails of any regular sized human and sent them reeling right into Stupid Town. But not Edgar. He just grunted a bit and grinned his gapped teeth wide and proud at Mikey. Before Leanna could even offer up her twisted idea of coaching to her man, Mikey took Edgar's gloating as an opportunity and chopped him right in the neck with the edge of his hand. THWOCK. It sounded like something got dislodged nice and good. His larynx? His Adam's apple? It was enough for the big-dicked lurchasaurus to grab his throat and squeal like a skidded tire through his yapper.

"Finish him! Now!" Leanna yelled as she jumped up and down way too excitedly.

Miss Fanny shot a death stare at Leanna and snarled to her hooker throng, "When Edgar is done with the meathead, kill the fucking pighsit out of this bitch."

Some of the hookers locked and loaded. Others nodded or grinned or chuckled. If Mikey did kill this dude, getting out of here was a slim kind of pickings at this point. Something else had to be done.

As Edgar staggered backwards, Mikey regained a visual on the broken champagne bottle and snatched it up. He pummeled Edgar in the face with one good swipe, shredding the bouncer's cheek and leaving globs of blood on the sharp ends of the dead sparkling wine container. After a moment of genuine, foreign shock to his system at such an attack, Edgar regrouped and charged Mikey, wailing the wail of a damaged kettle spout. Mikey took two shots from the frightened yet livid monster - one to the gut and one to face. Sucking for air and seeing stars, Mikey instinctively ducked and successfully dodged a third blow that would have almost certainly put his lights out for good. As he rose again, he realized he was still holding the champagne bottle and instinctively thrust it forward with the force of a battering ram. It invaded Edgar's lower torso and lodged itself in there with a splish-splash of crimson dotting Mikey's naked body: face, pecs, abdomen, pubes. The works. He looked like a Jackson Pollock painting if it were hanging in the backroom of a butcher's shop. Mikey and Edgar exchanged a brief look between each other and both their eyes widened. They each reached for the bottle and Edgar was a hair faster. Mikey pushed back hard to prevent Edgar from pulling the bottle out and weaponizing it against him. The struggle quickly slid to Edgar's favor, so Mikey had to break the one unwritten rule guys try like hell to never, ever violate.

He purposely kneed Edgar right in his free-hanging nutsack.

Turned out, Edgar was no eunuch. In fact, he was the exact opposite of a eunuch. Whatever that was. Some sort of sasquatch maybe? Regardless, Edgar folded like a piece of paper at an origami convention and as he went down, Mikey wrenched the bottle from his innards and caused them to spill outwards in a steamy heap of gut soup. Resisting the urge to be transfixed by the warm floor gore, Mikey kicked Edgar in the junk again and shoved the bloody bottle into the bouncer's crotch, sealing his dick and balls in a glass prison of broken knives.

And then he twisted. Multiple times. With the force of a thousand cuckolded suns from a thousand cuckolded galaxies.

"Nobody fucks my girl from now on but me."

Mikey roared that statement as Edgar's dick, balls, scrotum, gooch, and any and all hair down there sloughed off inside the broken and now no longer see-through champagne bottle. Mikey looked to Leanna, bloody and breathing heavy. She'd never been so turned on in her life. It almost made her want to go monogamous right then and there.

Wow. What the fuck, Mikey. Hot god damn, I say.

The circular gaggle of armed naked hookers exchanged confused glances. Some cried for Edgar. Others looked to Miss Fanny. Was this in the cards? What do they do now? Miss Fanny visibly seethed, her nostrils flaring. It looked like she was about to blow her stack but then all went calm on her person. After a sharp inhale, she addressed her two now unwelcome guests quite evenly.

"Well played, young man. That was an unexpected turn of events but still a welcome one regardless. Congratulations on becoming my new bouncer and bitch boy. You'll enjoy it if you just let yourself get into the spirit of the role."

Leanna still faced towards Mikey as Fanny babbled on and hadn't yet turned to regard her the entire time. She couldn't see Leanna subtly and quietly pull Miss Fanny's little .22 Magnum Sidewinder out of her vagina.

Old bag never even knew it was even missing.

Mikey's eyes bulged out of his head and whimpered. Leanna winked at him. He was such a sweet boy. She almost felt guilty about exposing him to all this violence. *Almost.*

Miss Fanny smiled and blew a kiss to Mikey. "Don't cry, little fella. You were a great lay. Stupid as hell, but a great lay. As I said, I'll let you stay on as my personal boot licker, bouncer, and even busboy. They make great tips. Better than a bullet to the face, right?"

Miss Fanny's nipples got hard when she was threatening someone. *Small world*, Leanna mused. That aside, nobody talks about Mikey like that except for Leanna. She was now fuming, shoulders moving up and down noticeably. And Miss Fanny soon noticed. But what she didn't notice or even hear was Leanna cocking the hammer on Fanny's Sidewinder ever so slowly in the midst of Miss Fanny's otherwise delectable tirade. *I kinda liked you. You could'a been my mom in another life, bitch.*

"And you, twat. You can be our little gateway bitch. I'll let you service every two-bit redneck trucker and dirty Mexican gangster that fumble-fucks their way in here until your nasty, Venus flytrap pussy falls right the fuck off. Deal? Turn the fuck around when I'm talking to you!"

One Shot. One kill.

Leanna whipped around, aimed as best she could, and shot Miss Fanny right in the throat, a tiny hole in the front and a small hurricane of blood and throat muscle in the back. It was a heavenly opera of carnage to Leanna's eyes and ears. Fanny's shotgun went off wild, hitting an armed hooker nearby right in the face, exploding her poor moneymaker into shredded pieces of flesh and bone, killing her dead where she stood.

Ha! Bullseye, bitch. Holy fucking shit.

"Deal," Leanna retorted, trying to keep cool on the outside.

Mikey and Leanna grabbed their stuff and hauled ass for the door, taking advantage of the confusion and shock that had set in amongst assemblage of hookers. But it didn't last long. Once one of them opened fire, it was full-on checkout time. The naked lovers ran like hell from a hailstorm of bullets. Leanna fired back as Mikey slung her over his shoulder. Leanna managed to hit three hookers out of the numberless horde pursuing them. One got it in the stomach, one in the thigh, and the last one square in the chest. *Last bullet*. She fired and the final round hit nothing and no one. *Fuuuuck.*

"Run faster, Mikey! Fucking run!" She threw the used-up Sidewinder at another hooker, knocking her out cold on her feet. The hooker ran a few more steps before planting her face into the cold, hard chessboard tile floor.

One naked armed hooker managed to hit Leanna in the shoulder, who immediately screamed in equal amounts of frustration and hurt.

"Fucking shitty Texas hookers!"

Mikey busted through the front door, a bleeding, cursing Leanna on his shoulder with an army of naked prostitutes chasing them, gunshots filling the air in a symphony of early morning gusto.

Mikey threw Leanna through the open passenger window of his Trans Am and slid over the hood on his naked ass, making a terrible streaking sound. He got in, started it up and peeled out as fast as he could as bullets hit his car in several places.

Leanna glanced back at the mob of sex workers getting smaller and smaller in the rear window. She squeezed her bloody shoulder and bellowed. That was way closer than any other jam she'd ever found herself in before. Her adrenaline was still pumping from landing that shot on Miss Fanny.

"Did you see that shit? One in a fucking million."

"She wasn't that far away, Lee."

"You're welcome, asshole. Jesus fucking Christ."

"And you're welcome, too."

He was right. He got them out of there. She would have just shot it out with those hookers and probably ended up deader than Dillinger. It sounded like a pretty rad death, though.

"Thanks for getting us out of there. That was fucking crazy."

Mikey did a double take. A slight one, but a double take, nonetheless. Was he surprised she knew how to say thank you? It couldn't be that simple. She'd said thank you to him before, for sure.

Have I?

THIRTY-SIX...

Teena went to a deep, dark place, holding Della for so long. Beyond Ronnie. All the way down to the day she found *him*...

Wallis lay dead on the floor in the kitchen, strangled. Red marks and purple bruises marred his neck. Glasses askew, tongue flopped out. Eyes wide open. The back door to the house was busted open. Dishes and glasses broken all over the floor. An empty jewelry box lay open next to Wallis's dead hand.

She wanted to make it look like a robbery. Well, it was. A different kind of robbery altogether. I wonder if she ever realized that.

The sound of the front door opening and someone coming in. The sound of Teena returning home from a long day of work at that accursed cannery. The place might as well have been called Insult to Injury Canned Foods.

"I'm home, baby."

I was so looking forward to one of Wallis's signature foot rubs that night. He knew all the right pressure points.

"Wallis? Are you here?"

After a moment, Teena made her way into the kitchen and saw poor Wallis. She fell to her knees and inched her way over to him, over broken plates and glasses, sobbing like a wild animal. She grabbed him and held onto him tight, mumbling something incoherent and rocking him back and forth like a newborn babe.

~666~

Teena laid on Della's bed, covered in blood. Wallis and Ronnie were nestled up to her on either side, moaning and drooling black goo.

Lloyd Bob and J.D. Tyson were now part of the fold. Their badly devoured and broken bodies swiveled and creaked all over the place as they ambled and shambled around the room, bumping into each other. Two half-eaten turkey legs with slack jaws and hungry mouths.

Della Suzanne remained dead on the floor next to the bed. No reanimation for her.

In her left hand, Teena vigorously rubbed the lock of blond hair as she hummed in between sobs.

I'll find her. I'll find her. I'll find her.

A rooster crowed somewhere outside. Teena finally let loose a scream of savage sorrow and rage.

I'll find her.

PART FOUR

THE INEVITABLE
DEATH OF LEANNA
FORSYTHE

Dear Fucking Diary,

I see it all now. Ronnie won't return my calls. Teena's never at home. I think the cops are coming for me. They sold me out. Do they know about Wallis? Of all the fucking things... I told my shrink he had a tiny dick and his wife never loved him. I think he's going to kill himself. I'm not going to run. I'll let them take me. They'll go back to their lives, thinking they won. The bitch is gone, right? She's gotta die. She will die. And Mikey will help.

-LF

THIRTY-
SEVEN...

Fanny's Hot Box was officially closed for the season. And probably every season after that. The cops had it all taped up, doing their cop-ass things.

Richards pulled up, got out, and surveyed the situation, hands firmly in his jacket pockets.

"What in the name of Linda Lovelace..."

He waited for a window of opportunity and when it came a few moments later, he walked right in through the front door when no one was looking.

The main party room slash lobby was a disaster area to put it kindly. Smashed liquor bottles, spent ammo, holes all over the place. Bloodstains on the pink upholstery. Three dead hookers. The one Leanna got in the stomach bled out before anyone could arrive on the scene. The one Miss Fanny accidentally face-erased with her shotgun whilst in the throes of death. And the one Leanna cold cocked with the Sidewinder suffered massive head trauma and never woke up again. Oh yes, and a dead Miss Fanny was lined up and sheeted next to them as well.

"It's a goddamn skankpocalypse. Fuck me jogging..."

A baby-faced and overeager uniformed cop with a squinty frown bounded over to Richards and put a firm hand on him.

"Out. Now."

"Hold on, hold on. I'm a private investigator hired by one of these young lady's fine folks to find out what they're doing here. I gotta know if she's one of the unfortunate dead."

"Wait outside and we'll talk to you shortly."

"You can just say fuck off instead of all of that fancy shit."

"Let's go, Rockford."

As the cop tried to drag Richards out, one of the dead hookers, covered in a clean white sheet, sat straight up. Gnashing. Snarling. Growling. Then, the other two dead hookers did the same thing. And then Miss Fanny.

Black goo seeped through their once pristine death coverings before they slid off completely. Hooker zombies. They smelled fucking horrible. Richards winced at the stench. Rotten fish and roadkill slathered with fresh human shit. *This couldn't be actual... Could it?*

"I seen this somewhere before," Richards frowned as he scratched his head.

A nebbish medical examiner with thick, horrendously smudged glasses and a combover on disability tried to communicate with one of the dead hookers who now happened to be shaking all over like a crackhead in Iceland. He was rewarded with her teeth to his face as she dug in and ripped a chunk out of him with a wet, papery tear that made Richards gag. The unfortunate chap screamed a high-pitched yelp and ran straight into a wall, knocking himself out just in time to avoid feeling anything as the very same hooker zombie pounced on him and devoured the rest of his face like it was a big, saggy, raw chicken thigh filled with warm strawberry jam.

"Goddamn, son." Richards reached for his gun. Accuracy was going to be a big selling point here. He thanked the Lord he had renewed his permit and visited the range a few weeks ago. Sharnell insisted a refresher course for his rusty ass. Another reason to love that damn woman.

As Richards armed himself, so did the overeager cop that was ready to boot Richards from the premises. For some reason his hands were all shaky now like he was scared of something. All four dead ladies rose up and laid siege to the panicked cops, coroners, firemen, and EMT's. Some first responders tried to run away in a screaming panic, while a handful cops tried to shoot them with terrible, frightened aiming. A few of them managed to shoot each other, which kind of defeated the whole purpose. Others succeeded in shooting some of the zombies. But they weren't going down just yet.

"Head shots, boys!" Richards called out to them in a firm but even tone. *Just like Patton on the battlefield*, he thought to himself.

The squinty cop aimed for the head of one of the hooker zombies and pulled the trigger. BLAM! The zombie folded in half and splatted to the floor as the bullet punched into its rotten watermelon of a head then exited with a weak queef out the other end. One down.

"I got one!" The squinty cop squeaked with equal parts fear and excitement.

No sooner than the excitable boy of a cop had celebrated his sharpshooting ability, another hooker zombie was on him lickety-split, ripping him to pieces with its ratty, broken fingernails by starting with some left side shoulder meat action. A chunk of skin and sinewy tissue ripped off his frame with the same sound a whistling roman candle makes when it goes off. Or that could have just been the cop screaming. Or maybe both.

"Aw shit, son. You had potential." Richards shot the second hooker zombie in the head, this one exploding on impact. A shower of flimsy skull and soupy brains painted the room and Ricky's wardrobe. Without missing a beat, he head-shotted the squinty cop next. The bullet rocketed into the guy's right looking hole and caved in part of his skull. As he plopped to the ground, he reached for his eye socket in the most delayed of a reaction Richards had ever witnessed. He laughed at the very notion of it as another one of his bullets decimated the medical examiner's chewed-up cranium. He reloaded hastily and hummed Clarence Carter's "Strokin'" as the other cops began to shake and convulse from their hooker zombie bite wounds. He took aim five times and their skulls imploded one-by-one similar to someone shoving a vacuum up their asses and ramming it all the way past their uvula.

Ain't no coming back from that shit.

The last rando hooker zombie and Miss Fanny herself went for Richards at the same time, teeth gnashing and spitting black goo everywhere. Their growls and screams sounded like two cats fighting to the death in an empty hospital hallway. Feral and hollow.

Richards managed to take out the one rando hooker zombie with a perfectly placed bullet to the head. He could have sworn she let out a disappointed grunt as she hit the floor. But how can you grunt when you have no face? *That a skill only the sexy undead got?*

He turned his aim to Miss Fanny, his brow a-drip with sweat, and CLICK. Out of ammo.

Well, shit.

Fanny pounced on him and tried to rip his face off with her putrid, gore-stained teeth and her cracked, jangly fingernails. Or were those her finger bones? Ricky was damned if he was going to find out the hard way. He spotted her throat hole from Leanna's bullet, shoved a couple fingers in there and tugged them all around, ripping her neck and lower jaw apart completely. Teeth cascaded into his mouth. He spit them back at her reflexively as her tongue flicked out and caressed his face just so with a wet, sticky *squuiiisshhh*. Richards found her upper spine with his fingers, grabbed a hold of it with his whole hand and snapped it in two, her head tumbling off her shoulders like a cantaloupe rolling off a produce stand on a brisk autumn day. *Thunk-thunk-thunk.*

Richards got up, breathing heavy. He couldn't remember whether he had taken his blood pressure medication. He definitely took his cholesterol medication. But his blood pressure pills? He hadn't the foggiest. He went to take his pulse, but decayed gunk covered his digits. He shook his hands in a mild panic, trying to get Fanny's neck goo off his fingers.

"Fucking Calgon take me away."

He double checked to see if anyone was still alive. Negatory. All of his allies had "bitten" the dust. Hard. They were strewn about here and there and everywhere. And back to here again. There were too many other victims to headshot. This called for a broader, less precise approach.

~666~

Richards strolled outside, cigarette in mouth, Zippo in one hand. Covered in rancid zombie chitterlings. He lit his cig, headed to his car, popped the trunk, and pulled out a can of gas.

A few surviving cops and EMT's caught on to what he was doing and tried to stop him.

"Look, boys. You seen what happened in there. Anyone got a reason as to why this shit should stay standing?"

No one responded.

"That is *exactly* what I thought. One side, now."

~666~

Back inside Fanny's, the remaining fresh victims started to squirm. Soon it would be up-and-walking-around time for them.

No can do, amigos.

Richards took his trusty gas can and hastily doused the whole place the best he could with the flammable liquid as he sang a few verses of "Stagger Lee" before tossing his lit Zippo in an especially saturated spot. The magenta settee that sat in the middle of the foyer. It was fucking ugly, Ricky determined.

You go first.

And so it did.

~666~

Fanny's Hot Box was now as advertised. The firemen were dead, though. So were a lot of the EMT's. And most of the cops.

A naked hooker, the one hit in the face with Leanna's gun, sat in the back of an ambulance, a blanket draping her, partially concealing her Disney cartoon tattoos and uncomfortably oversized fake boobs. She said her name was Daisy. *Of course her name was Daisy.*

Richards strolled up to her and smiled.

"Hey, pretty girl. Mind telling me what happened here?"

"I already talked to the cops. What the hell just happened in there? Is everyone alright?"

"No. Everyone is *not* alright. That right there was what you would call an outbreak of the undead. I actually saw it yesterday but didn't want to believe it at the get go. Now I do. Hindsight, they say. You better believe it. Know what I mean?"

"—What?"

"I just need you to tell me who started all this, sweetheart. Can you do that?"

I already know who done did it, I just wanna hear it from the hot-ass horse's mouth.

Richards handed her a folded Benjamin Franklin. Daisy snatched it with a sniff.

"Some uppity jezebel and her jock boyfriend showed up a few hours before sunup, talking smack to everyone. Saying how they could screw better than anyone else here. Miss Fanny was about to rob them and toss their behinds back outside without a pot to pee in when all the sudden they started passing around this purple stuff."

"Purple stuff? Elaborate, you sweet little lady of the night, you."

"I dunno. Never seen it before. But pretty much everyone took it and before anyone knew which way was up, we were having the biggest orgy in the history of creation. Everyone was doing everyone, over and over again. It was like molly, Spanish Fly, cocaine, and Jesus H. Christ's personal supply of Mary Magdalene's titty milk all rolled into one."

"You don't say. And I assume it's all gone."

Daisy rummaged around underneath her ambulance blanket and pulled out an empty purple pouch.

"I kept one of the bags. I think it smells nice."

Richards took it from Daisy. He gave her another hundred. "You mind?"

"Doesn't smell *that* good."

"Thank you, darling."

Richards swaggered over to his car. He took a sniff from the bag, squinted hard and grimaced, his neck muscles tensing up fiercely. He stared off into the endless horizon of the I-10. Westbound, of course. They were out there. Headed straight for Tucson and Drakesworth's lab. It was time to close the distance between himself and his prey. Sharnell would be there soon. Everything was set for the perfect ambush. If he hadn't just finger-fucked the melting madam of the house's spinal cord, Richards would've danced a jig.

Instead, he just settled for a long drag off his cigarette and the peace of mind of knowing Leanna Forsythe would soon die a horrible death at the hands of someone. *Anyone.* It was all just a matter of time now and he'd be there to pick up the pieces and collect more than just a goddamn tip.

Our big payday is comin' baby, just you wait.

THIRTY-
EIGHT...

In a distant land, far from anywhere she recognized, Leanna had died. She knew she was dead because her skin was rotting. She could smell the dust. Seeping from her every pore. Ejecting from her nostrils, oozing from her eyes, running from her ears. It smelled like the dust for sure, but also like formaldehyde. Then her skin healed, reforming itself. But to a plastic, artificial degree. She felt her body being taxidermized. Her mother's voice inside her head saying something about how they could be together now. She would keep Leanna in the living room. She'd let her see her father from time to time. It was a hideous tone, a tone she had never heard from her mother before. A mix of lies and sincerity. A mocking admission of love. Another sound drowned out her mother. Leanna's deafening sobs of regret and sorrow. Then her mother laughed at her. At her weakness. Her vulnerability. Leanna looked back at her skin and saw it rot away again. Melt down into the dirt, leaving her a drooping cadaver of tissue and sinew and bone. She was now no longer on the ground. She was in her mother's hand. A giant hand. And it was closing in on her for good...

~666~

Leanna woke to her reality, unimpressive as it was. She and Mikey were holed up in a shitty motel room. The kind where the TV was bolted to the floor on a metal stand and the sheets looked like they hadn't been bleached since the Carter administration.

Leanna had poured herself into a pair of tight jeans and not much more. She had a large bandage wrapped snug around her shoulder meat. A faint blood spot seeped through ever so slightly. She had the photo of her father that she swiped from Teena's chest earlier resting in the limp hand that belonged to her shot-up shoulder.

Dad... What would you do right now? How the hell did you live with her?

Mikey flipped through channels on the shitty TV as Leanna nursed a bottle of Bowman's vodka. Leanna took one last long swig and fell back against the shitty pillows on her shitty side of the bed. She leaned over as best she could and kissed Mikey on the small of his back.

"That tickles. How's the shoulder?"

"Ask my vodka. That Doctor should be tarred and feathered."

"He's a vet, Lee. What did you want him to do?"

"He asked me what kind of breed I was."

"Well, I thought that was funny."

Leanna spit vodka in his face. Mikey wiped it away with a chuckle.

"He was super old, that's for sure. Plus he ain't seen anything as hot as you in a while, I bet. I think it was just his way around a pickup line."

"Fucking veterinarian humor."

"You good to head out in the morning?"

"We're so close, baby. I can feel it, touch it, smell it all at once. Soon we can do whatever we want with ourselves. New life, new name, new everything. Ain't no one gonna catch us. They're all too busy killing each other."

"—Is that a yes?"

"Is what a yes?"

"I was thinkin'—"

"About time."

"Maybe we could try the—"

Here it comes. Bout to get Reverse Bollywooded up in here.

"...porno films. On account of all this dust we got...and we're gonna have. Could really clean up and be famous at the same time. And we ain't gotta do no movie movies, neither. Just long as we're together, that's all I care about. We could do themed compilations. Cowboys. Ninjas. Oil barons. Frenchmen. The works. What do you think?"

Leanna was impressed and a little titillated. Could be fun. But monogamous porn? Who was that for? Mormons? It sounded too safe. But still...

"Got it all figured out already, huh?" Leanna grumbled.

"I don't know. Maybe." Mikey sounded honest. Vulnerable. Even more than normal.

"Porno star ain't first on my list, but it ain't last neither. No one'd be able to follow us while we're on the dust. Shit, we'd be the main event from Miami to Vegas."

"Hell yeah. That's what I was thinkin'."

Leanna pulled out a purple pouch. "What else you thinking?" She smiled seductively.

"But we only got two left. And you're a purple heart recipient, baby."

"Only need *one* to show that Drakesworth fella."

Mikey tossed the remote and grabbed the vodka from Leanna.

"I believe you might be what they call an addict, ma'am."

"Shut up and let me fuck you proper, porno star."

Mikey took a pull of the vodka and kissed her while it was still in his mouth, making a sloppy two-way vodka kiss.

Leanna could get used to this kind of excess. Maybe adult film star wasn't such a bad thing. They'd need new names, of course. Mikey could try out something meaty. Hunky. An eye-rolling pun in there somewhere. She'd go by something along the lines of Maxine Horner. It sounded retro. Sophisticated. Yet still sexy. She'd have to workshop it.

Vodka kisses and porno names. Things were looking up.

Velma Hipsway? Kelly Kinks? Cool names for a chick seemed harder if you didn't want to go the obvious way. As she straddled Mikey, both of their pants undone and pulled down just enough for docking, she grabbed the vodka and poured it all over themselves, returning Mikey's wet kiss with her own.

Teena ain't never had this before. I'd bet my fucking life on it.

THIRTY-NINE...

Tag Team Tacos. A garish, tacky tourist trap eatery off I-10 in New Mexico. The sign had a pro-wrestler wearing a jalapeno sombrero and a championship belt made of tacos. Crunchy shells.

I wonder if they ate here on their way to a payday at my expense. Did they enjoy the tacos? Maybe they had burritos...

Teena was parked off to the side and near the back, away from the crowd of customers. She had a plate of tacos and was trying to feed it to her undead friends through the bars on the door. The horse trailer rumbled and shook. More moans and groans. It sounded like there was a whole army of the dead back there.

Della's face had completely overtaken Ronnie in her mind's eye. It followed her every thought like an albatross named Damocles. She wasn't sure killing Leanna would even do anything to soothe it. Maybe she had to kill Mikey, too. He probably had nothing to do with it. But he was an enabler. Enablers had to die as well. They just had to. She wished she had something more substantial for her children, but she was caught with little else to offer them. No stray men wandering around. Just families with their lobotomized male units driving them to their next bout of ennui. They wouldn't stray over here to hit on her. Not in front of the children. For the first time in a long time, she wished her perfume had a much longer range. She placed a soft hand on one of the bars. Rotting hands reached back and caressed her fingers. It felt so nice to be wanted. Appreciated.

"This is all I have, darlings. I'm sorry."

The growls persisted, more agitated now. Dead hands retreated back into the shadows of the trailer.

"Fine."

Teena tried a bite and gagged. It tasted worse than the tacos at Jack-In-The-Box. Just hideous.

How the devil is this place still in business?

She tossed the taco plate behind her and looked around for something, anything, to feed them.

A well-fed cat skittered by her car, collar bell jingling. She knew the look in its eyes. Freedom at last from its banal human family and the confines of a suffocating station wagon.

"Here, kitty kitty."

~666~

At the front of the establishment, Ricky Richards pulled in and parked up front. He got out, stretched, and tried to light a cigarette. No Zippo anymore. He tossed the cigarette, cursing under his breath. He should have swiped a book of matches from Fanny's Hot Box. Distractions notwithstanding. *Oh well.*

He spotted the car and horse trailer out of the corner of his eye. The trailer was rocking back and forth with great strength and purpose.

"The hell...?"

He crept his way over there, pulling his gun out gradually, looking around to see if anyone was watching or looking in his direction. No one. Busy stuffing their faces with shitty tacos. As he got closer, he heard a cat growling and then screaming. And then nothing. It was gradually adding up. The whorehouse. The ambush at mommy's house. Now this. They came in threes, right?

Well, I think this right here is number fucking three.

He made a wide berth as he came around the corner of the trailer and aimed his gun at Teena as soon as he saw her.

Yup. Numero three.

"Well, I'll be the concubine of a shaolin monk..."

Teena seemed neither surprised nor frightened to see him again. Was that annoyance on her face? He had half a mind to pistol whip her. But what was in the trailer? And how many of those whats?

"Leanna hired you, didn't she?" Teena's voice was fighting any shred of emotion from infecting itself.

"Among other things. She never said you'd be packing two whacked-out crackheads ready to die for you."

"Those two...cavemen. You sent them?"

Ricky sighed at the reminder of Lloyd Bob and J.D. Tyson. "I sure did. And I see they didn't come as advertised. That's what I get for outsourcing my work yet again."

Teena tightened her mouth, fighting back tears.

"All I have to do is open this door—"

"I'd prefer it if you didn't."

"Give me one reason why I shouldn't."

"Now that I think of it, I reckon you're after her just as I am. You do want to kill her, I'm assuming?"

Teena didn't answer, just stared hard at him.

"I'll take that as a resounding yes."

Teena reached for the door to the horse trailer, keeping her eyes locked on Richards.

"Hold up, now. We don't want no Day of the Dead shootout at such a nice little taqueria. There're kiddos here, ma'am. They don't need to see that. And they don't need to see your voodoo bitch brains all over the asphalt, either."

Teena lowered her hand a little, still staring daggers at Richards. He had her now. He could just crater her head with one bullet. It would be a mess, though. Cops were behind him all over the place. One report of a gunshot at a taco stand directly ahead of them would be all they needed. No more favors. No more handshakes. He had to gut this one out with this crazy cat lady of the undead.

"I don't fashion myself a genius or nothing, but I think we should pool our resources until that crazy lil' strumpet has shuffled off her mortal coil. I mean, you've had some rough times getting to this point, some of them admittedly my doing. But hell, I've had a tough go of it, too. I literally just came from a flaming whorehouse of fucking doom. Zombie hookers and crazy fuck dust being the culprits."

Teena dropped her hand completely.

"My love potion..."

Love potion? Shit, more like sex crack.

"That shit's *yours*? Wow you two are something fucking else. How long this blood feud been going on?"

"She's using my dust on the uninitiated. Anyone not sworn in under the practice of voodoo that uses the dust are cursed to return as the undead after expiring."

"Yeah, like I said, I already fucking seen that shit. And that shit don't look like no voodoo I ever heard of, that's for goddam certain."

"You don't understand. She's trying to sell it to an established buyer who will then mass produce and distribute it all over the world. The last time I checked, the voodoo faithful didn't come anywhere near close to seven or eight billion souls. Once people figure out what it is, it won't be just junkies who will kill for it. Middle America will burn at the hands of sex-crazed soccer moms and fatally horny elderly war vets alike. It will be the true apocalypse."

"Well, shit. Don't you think we should be going, missy? I got a backup plan already in place and ahead of the curve."

"If you try anything, and I mean anything, and my sweet boys will have you for lunch. And you *will* still pay for what happened to my friend."

Shit. Her friend? What the fuck did those two shitdicks do? How the fuck did Sharnell make friends with them? He loved her mysterious nature most of the time, but not when it came to making sure the right person got whacked. That's a whole different world of math.

Richards spat on the ground near Teena.

"Sorry about that. What'd they do, anyhow?"

Teena balled up her fist. He could see she wanted to strike him bad. She soon relented, though. Richards chuckled and winked.

Aww. No fist fight. Whatever then.

"Follow me," Richards beckoned her.

Just then, a little freckled girl in a tracksuit and braided pigtails ran around the corner, sobbing.

"Jimmy Whiskers? Jimmy Whiskers! Have you seen my kitty, Sir Jimmy Whiskers? He wears a little jingly bell to protect him from evil!"

FORTY...

On the outskirts of Tucson itself, Mikey and Leanna pulled up to a massive brick warehouse with oodles of plate glass windows about ten feet from the ground. A handful of expensive cars dotted the parking lot about a hundred yards from the warehouse. They got out lackadaisically, eyeing the cars with a whistle. This was it. After everything they'd been through, making it to Tucson felt anticlimactic. No ambush. No pursuers. They were just there. It made Leanna wistful for just a bit of the bloodshed. Just a little. She took in the whole of the building and almost fell over backwards doing so.

"Holy fucking shit. We're here."

"Hoo! Think they'll let us buy that Beamer over there?"

"Already spending money we don't have yet, huh?"

"Wishful thinking. Beats a used car lot."

"This is definitely the place. It even smells like organized crime."

"Them sweet cars are a dead giveaway."

"Will you shut up about the fucking cars? Come on."

They made a beeline for the inside, stiffly arm-in-arm. Forcing themselves to be a loving, caring couple. Leanna knew they weren't fooling anyone. But it made her feel better.

Inside was a gigantic, fully automated production facility, unmistakably designed for mass-producing illicit narcotics. An army of factory workers and armed guards filled up the place. It looked like something right out of one of those horseshit 80s action movies Mikey insisted on making her watch. Or maybe it was 90s. He had a whole speech about the difference between decades that she refused to pay attention to. It *was* impressive to see something like that in person, though.

Not more than a minute of them being inside, a flood of suit-wearing security goons blocked their path. Well-dressed for sure. No cheap department store suits. And MP40's strapped to their shoulders from under their suit jackets. Smooth as fuck. It didn't intimidate Leanna. She'd been in a women's prison and turned down being a bitch to multiple murderous females despite the inevitable beatings for such defiance. This was nothing. Men pointing guns. Yawn.

"We have an appointment, boys," she announced with a sack full of pride.

"She speaks the truth. Let her pass," a booming voice said, cutting through the security and straight into Leanna and Mikey's ear drums. As the goons parted like the Red Sea, a huge and very burly man in an all-black suit and white turtleneck strolled up and grinned ear-to-ear. His voice was like listening to Barry White recite Shakespeare. The man himself. Drakesworth.

"Your odyssey has ended, my child. Take comfort in my facilities."

"That's one big motherfucker."

"He can hear you." Mikey warned.

"Oh. Right. That's one big motherfucker," she whispered this time.

"Was your journey arduous? Taxing?" Drakesworth asked with at least the faintest whiff of genuine interest on his lips.

"You could say that. Is it deal-making time yet?" Leanna was done wagging tongues with older wannabe authority figures. Her mom. Miss Fanny. That rat fuck Richards. This guy was boring her already.

"So soon after arriving she talks of business. So soon." Drakesworth looked to his men for a laugh as he smiled. They gave him a polite chuckle. Not too much. Just enough to stay employed and alive.

"What else are we gonna do? Go to the fucking movies?" Leanna said.

"If I could make one request, it's that you might refrain from such foul language in my place of business. Did your mother not teach you your rightful manners?"

"Uh, I wouldn't bring up her mother if I were you, sir. And I'm clearly not. As you can see," Mikey appealed to Drakesworth with arms crossed at his waist. Probably didn't want to make any sudden moves. Leanna was amused and impressed at the same time with her Mikey. All grown up now.

Drakesworth clicked his tongue inside his mouth. Was he tutting her? *Fuck. Him.*

"I was wondering who I'd see first: my sweet, vivacious Teena or her rambunctious offspring I've heard so much about."

"You know my mother? She fuck you or did she *fuck* you? Has to be one of the two."

Fucking hell. Is there one corner of this fucking planet that doesn't have the stink of Teena Forsythe on it?

Mikey tried in vain yet again to be the peacemaker. "Lee, don't tick this guy off, remember what Jiman—"

"Ah, Jiman. A colorful satellite distributor of mine. A little bit of a stereotypical Jamaican American, but he moves merchandise like no one's business. He spoke extremely highly of your...product."

"I goddamn hope so."

Drakesworth removed his sunglasses and lowered his booming voice a little. His eyes were steely grey and unflinching. Unblinking. Leanna wondered if the sunglasses were to keep people from freaking out during normal conversations with him. It made sense to her.

"If your product does what it's been claimed to do, I can guarantee you will become a very rich woman."

"Damn straight. How much?"

Drakesworth laughed heartily. "You are so funny, little Leanna. Before we can talk monetary compensation, we must test your product. Give us the night to thoroughly examine it and we will meet again on the morrow."

Leanna pulled her gun and pointed it at Drakesworth. His goons predictably drew their weapons on her in return.

"Of course it does what we say it does. We ain't just drove halfway across the country to a huge honking drug den with bullshit product. Give us our fucking money or so help me God I'll blast a hole through your bowling ball head."

"Lee! I'm sorry, Mr. Drakesworth, sir. She's been on edge a lot lately. She don't mean none of it, I swear."

"The fuck I don't."

She cocked the hammer. The goons tensed up, moving in closer.

"That's enough, boys. Put the guns down. She's just puffing her chest, so to speak and as it were."

"Am I?"

"Yes, you are."

"I should pull this here trigger just for sending those idiot brains after us at the truck stop. The fuck was that all about?"

"Dierks and Flavio were merely a test. To see if you could pass muster, as it were. If they were able to take the dust from you so easily, then what point would it be for me to go into business with you? You apparently passed with oh-so-flying colors in the end. So what exactly is the problem now?"

"You think that's some kinda good enough answer? I still got you in my crosshairs, asshole."

"Ah, I know what might help."

Drakesworth chuckled deep, snapped his fingers and one of his goons brought over a suitcase. He opened it and revealed it was stuffed with cash. Stacks of twenty-dollar bills wrapped nice and tight.

"Oh my Jesus. Lee! Put the gun down," Mikey pleaded.

Drakesworth pulled out a couple stacks from the briefcase and sniffed them with a smile.

"Ten thousand beautiful American dollars. A finder's fee for bringing it to me. Here. It's yours. Put down your firearm, take the money and have a wonderful evening out with your easily excitable boyfriend here. On me."

Leanna eyed the wads of cash and gritted her teeth. After an agonizing moment of tense silence, she put her gun down.

Drakesworth tossed her the cash and it landed at her feet. Leanna threw the dust pouch at Drakesworth's feet.

Fucking deal.

"That should be plenty."

"Excellent. That is just a fraction of what you will receive if the product is everything it should be. Be here tomorrow at 9 AM sharp and we will continue this riveting transaction."

Drakesworth let out a toothy grin as he finished speaking. He turned and walked back to whatever he was doing and dismissed his guards with a nonchalant wave of his hand.

Leanna and Mikey were left in stunned silence, ten grand at their feet. She wanted to shout back at Drakesworth. Get the last word. Something vulgar or witty. She had nothing, though. Ten grand just to have while they waited? It boggled her mind. Maybe it was the dust? Her senses did feel dulled ever since the Hot Box. Like her reaction time was on mute. Just enough to notice. She resolved to lay off the dust for a while. After tonight, of course.

After tonight.

~666~

Leanna and Mikey stumbled out of the warehouse into the blaring daylight, high-fiving and smacking each other on the ass. A wad of cash in each one of their hands, hooting and hollering at their inevitable windfall.

Across the street and for all intents and purposes invisible to the couple was Sharnell. A manifestation of seething anger and raw determination. All for her Ricky. Dressed head-to-toe in dark red leather. Killer boots to match. Hair pulled back into the tightest ponytail imaginable. The stylistic exact opposite of Ricky Richards. Love is blind they say and so it fucking seemed. She pulled out her phone and made a call.

"They're here... Yeah, I'm sure. Dumb and Dumber in the flesh... Warehouse fifteen miles out. Northside, just like you said...I know, baby... Me too... Just get here. I wanna kill this chick right now. Love you too... Bye."

She hung up and stared bullets at Mikey and Leanna as they got in their car and drove off.

"Soon, bitch. Soon."

FORTY-ONE...

Ricky Richards hung up his phone and hocked a fat, juicy loogie. *They were fucking there.* He felt useless all of a sudden. *He* should be there. Not wasting his time with this fucking mental patient. But Sharnell would keep an eye on them. He trusted her. She'd make sure they stay put. It was going to be okay.

It's gotta be okay. Ain't no time for nothing else.

His car, along with Teena's car and trailer, were parked in the back of the seediest motel on the planet. The Sho-N-Tel Motel near Deming, New Mexico.

Richards was in between their cars and Teena was up on the balcony, next to the open door leading to her room.

"And who was that?"

"Oh nothin'. Just my backup plan that's already there. She moves fast."

"Then we need to leave right now."

"Don't you worry, lady. I know a thing or two about drug lords and kingpins and such. I reckon they're gonna test it and make sure she ain't blowing bullshit up their ass. Ten tits on a hog says she'll be back in the morning to collect her reward for the fuck dust. Rest up and we'll leave after dark. Ain't too far, now."

"She'll conveniently leave out the fact that it's cursed for the uninitiated."

"I reckon so. Wouldn't you?"

"I wouldn't sell my private, ceremonial creations on the black market."

"Well, then there's your answer. Your daughter's a greedy bitch that don't give two shits about you. I don't even know you and I'm about ninety-nine percent sure that's an accurate assessment of your relationship with her. Am I wrong?"

Teena just hung her head.

"What the fuck did you do to piss off that girl so much?"

"It's a long story."

"That's how it always goes, I'm afraid. Fifteen, twenty grand don't seem like it's worth the trouble of driving all the way out to the goddamn Copper State and dealing with such unsavory sorts."

"Oh no, it's much more than that, Mr. Richards."

"Come again?"

"When I first concocted the dust, as it's called, I was a little more promiscuous. So was my husband. Derek."

She paused when she said his name. Was she going to cry? It skeeved Richard out. So fucking awkward. Maybe the dad was the key to all this shit. Poor guy got caught up in the middle of all this female fuckery and probably paid for it.

"We passed it around, stupidly. An extraordinarily rich man got wind of it and offered a huge sum of money for the formula. Needless to say, after the post-life seed effects started to surface, I refused any offers and we tried to reverse our mistake. I had to learn several different ways to destroy the brain and spinal column of many deceased former party friends of ours."

Yup. He paid for it.

"And your husband..."

"—That was a separate incident."

"Hoo-boy. You accidentally killed your hubby and now daughty dearest has got a lifelong vendetta out on you to make your existence a living shitpile. What a world, huh?"

"She doesn't know he died. I told her he left us."

"Ho-lee fuck. So I bet she's been searching for a dead man all these years. You are one cold, cold broad. Dear Lord in Heaven and such."

"She's beyond redemption."

"And so are you, I wager."

"And most likely you as well."

"Got me there. So how much money we talking here? Fifty grand? A hundred?"

"Millions."

Richards almost fell right on his ass.

"Huh?"

"Millions of dollars, Mr. Richards. Probably tens of millions in this day and age."

"Adjusted for inflation, sure."

Richards drifted his gaze off into the distance, clicking his tongue methodically. *Millions. Fucking millions.* His ship had come in, docked, and all the sailors were out getting their dicks wet. All he had to do was swoop in and take it from Leanna.

It can't be this easy. I mean, it just can't. Can it?

"Don't get any ideas. This dust cannot be left in the hands of the uninitiated. It's ceremonial and needs to stay that way. I perverted it when I was young and ignorant and now I'm paying for my transgressions."

"But you're still gonna kill your daughter, right? And them boys you got chained up in that horse buggy are part of that plan? You are seriously fucked up in the ol' skull, missy."

Teena sniffed away some tears.

"Maybe so. Goodnight, Mr. Richards. The shadows will be here soon, and I must rest."

"Yeah. Okay. Whatever the fuck that means. See you soon."

Teena retreated to her room and shut the door. As soon as she was out of sight, Richards pulled out his phone and texted someone.

FORTY-TWO...

Mikey and Leanna chose to party in a desolate, run-down strip club called the Tumbleweed Supper Lounge. There was no supper to be had inside, though. The main event was two skeevy dancers rotating on the stage over and over again to the same shitty house music. There were only a few other sad sack patrons besides Mikey and Leanna. Also, an old Japanese bartender with an eye patch and a ponytail and a DJ who looked like someone dug up Tiny Tim's corpse and put a fake mustache on him.

Leanna didn't care about the ambience or lack thereof. She was already drunk as shit and dead set on celebrating their new life. A life of doing whatever the fuck they wanted, whenever they wanted. No jail. No begging for favors. None of it. Mikey had a drink in hand but looked sober and annoyed, trying desperately not to enable Leanna any more today. He'd come around. Leanna would make him have fun tonight.

"Start drinkin', bitch! We're celebrating. Whoooooo!"

"Yeah, Lee. I'm drinking. Calm down."

"Calm down? Fuck you. This is it, baby! We won! Game fucking over!"

"Not yet. We still got tomorrow. Then we win. You should slow down. Pace yourself, babe."

Leanna threw her beer in Mikey's face. *What the fuck was with him? Along for the ride until now? The fuck has changed? If*

219

anything, he should be the one partying his face off. He escaped death like multiple times on the way here. That shit was old hat for Leanna.

"Fuck you, I'm gonna have fun tonight," she shouted at him. *Alcohol shouts. Gotta love 'em.*

Leanna jumped onto the stage, next to the skanky stripper putting on a pathetic show. Leanna ground up against her and began undressing. The other patrons started to come alive at this display. Mikey was turning red. From embarrassment. From anger. Take your pick. Like it fucking mattered. *Goddamn buzzkill in tight, form-fitting t-shirts.*

"Lee! Get down from there. They're gonna kick us out."

"Aw, you don't wanna be here no how. Go back to the hotel and watch your cartoons, baby."

Leanna was almost completely naked at that point, just in her purple G-string and high heels. The whole place was up at the stage now, dancing and handing cash to Leanna, who tucked it all in her panty strings. A handful of people from outside came in and joined the commotion on top of it all.

The only person not enjoying themselves was Mikey. And it bothered Leanna. A lot.

No dust tonight. He don't deserve it. Or me.

FORTY-THREE...

Teena's room was dark and empty. It looked a lot like the shitty motel room Leanna and Mikey were in earlier. The front door flew open with a hard-booted kick. Richards aimed his gun around the room, searching for a target. No one home. Something felt off about it, though. It gave him a slight case of the heebie-jeebies. Richards shook off a chill and swore under his breath.

He couldn't believe he'd been dumb enough to think she was gonna team up with him to kill anyone, let alone Leanna. Not after what those two fuckheads did to her piece of Austin pussy. Maybe he should've apologized. *Hindsight alert*. Although, the irony of him being annoyed at her double-cross while he was attempting to double-cross her was not lost on him.

He spit on the threshold to her room and holstered his gun.
Now I'm the one picking up the rear. Aw, fuckin' hellfire...

~666~

Richards ran up to the back of the horse trailer. It was still there. Maybe she was, too.

221

Son of a bitch. Son of a bitch. Please be here, godammit.

He peeked in and saw nothing but dried blood and guts. And a cat collar with a bell. No zombies in sight, though. They were gone for sure. No ambush, no deadly double-cross. She was just gone.

She must really wanna kill that little ray of sunshine more than anything in this whole wide world. Double-talkin' voodoo bitch.

~666~

A green and yellow eighteen-wheeler with the words "SHAKIN' BACON" plastered on the side lumbered down I-5 in the fast lane. It passed a sign that said "TUCSON - 120".

Teena relaxed comfortably in the passenger seat, eyes closed and humming. Driving the rig was a surly, weathered old man with a dirty VFW cap and a plaid dress shirt, complete with oil-stained khakis and orange crocs. Good old Vernon. He introduced himself to Teena just that way. *Good Old Vernon, at your service.* Teena thought it was the cutest thing she'd seen or heard in years. Reminded her of what Ronnie might look like if he'd made it to old age.

"You sure your ponies are okay back there? They sounded awful strange earlier. You know, I could'a helped you load 'em up if you just..." Vernon's voice had a permanent tone of inquisitiveness about it. Perpetually asking a question out loud, regardless of whether it really was a question or not.

"Not to worry, Vernon, my darling. They're just fine back there. They enjoy the occasional quiet, private moment with their mommy."

"Whatever you say. Now where was this horse show again? Good Old Vernon'll get you there no problem ma'am."

As soon as Vernon finished speaking, he sniffed the air sharply.

"Say, what's that perfume you're wearing? It *is* you, right? Sure ain't me, last time I checked."

Teena just smiled and inhaled deep. She was outrunning the darkness. It wouldn't catch her. Not now. Not when she was so close. She had time.

FORTY-FOUR...

Leanna and Mikey stood in front of Drakesworth and a small army of his goons. Leanna was hungover like the dickens while Mikey remained completely uninterested, staring at his shoes.

Shouldn't have had that last absinthe chaser. Fuck my head; body and soul.

"So, your product was quite impressive," Drakesworth admitted.

"You don't say."

"I had quite the night last night."

"I bet you did."

"And you are quite sure there are no hidden side effects, correct?"

"Far as I know. Not a one."

"And she would know," Mikey mumbled under his breath.

"Quiet," Leanna snapped at him.

"Excellent. From my calculations, you are deserving of one point three million dollars today and once we are up and running on a regular basis, you will receive a monthly payment of fifty thousand dollars. Provided that business remains healthy, of course."

Leanna fell to the ground, gobsmacked. Almost crying. Her expectations were beyond shattered, every piece sent into orbit around Saturn. She could buy anything. Happiness. Love.

Revenge. Indifference. Sloth. Sex. It was all for sale now. Her prior hopes and dreams seemed laughably small in comparison. What a difference a day makes. Even Mikey's eyes widened a little, but she knew he was mentally checked out at this point. She'd get him to come back around. Eventually.

His loss if he don't cheer the fuck up and soon.

"Congratulations, little Leanna. Your ship has arrived. I hope we can maintain a successful professional relationship. Depending on business, we can hold an annual meeting to discuss any profit increases for you and your friend here."

"Can we just go home? Please?" Mikey was now in full-on whining pup mode, and it was nails on a chalkboard to Leanna.

"What the fuck's wrong with you? This is what we've been waiting for!"

"It's what *you've* been waiting for. So I guess you don't need me anymore."

"That ain't true and you know it. We been through a lot together. And you ain't never turned your back on me, not ever. I don't forget that shit. Just lighten up, baby."

"Do you love me?"

Goddamn it. There it was. That question again. The question she'd avoided most in her life so far. Teena tried to push it on her constantly. It never stuck. She felt this one, though. She knew Mikey needed it. She was afraid of what her kneejerk of a conscience thought of it, though.

"What?"

"Do you love me? I wanna hear you say it."

"What the fuck are you doing?"

"I just need to hear it once. That's all. Can you even do that?"

"Now's not the time for this shit. We'll talk about it later."

"Whatever. Can we just go, like right now please?"

"Fine. Alright, Mr. Drakesworth, that sounds like a plum deal. Shake on it?"

Drakesworth smiled all his teeth as he extended his hand. "Shake, indeed. Thank you, Miss Forsythe."

One of Drakesworth's goons came over and handed Leanna a sweet-looking black industrial briefcase.

Nice material. The professionalism don't stop around here. I like it.

"You may count it here, if you like," Drakesworth invited with a polite wave.

Leanna opened it up and marveled at the full mound of cash. This time it was all one-hundred-dollar bills. She cursed excitedly under her breath. She was gonna sell that bitch's house and build a goddamn palace over top of it. A God. Damned. Palace.

"I trust you, guy. That is, if we're to have a professional business relationship, as you said."

"I like you already, Leanna. You've got, what's the word? Spunk."

"In more ways than one," Mikey quipped.

The front doors swung open and Richards and Sharnell, armed to the teeth, rushed in. Sharnell cursed a blue streak in both English and Spanish.

Unfuckingbelievable.

Of all the people in the world. How the hell did he get here? Was he following them the whole time? She dreaded asking the one question that dominated her mind at that moment.

Did he even kill her?

"Now, don't make me tell her to start shootin', 'cuz she *kills* in both languages too, amigos."

"Ah, the young lovers. Almost right on schedule," Drakesworth said.

"What in the stupid fucking hell are you doing here? I already paid you." Leanna was one more outrage away from opening fire without nary a thought of the consequences. It was starting to smell like a double-cross and that was her gimmick.

"You paid me? You rootin' tootin' two-crossing bitch. Failed to tell me your mama wasn't alone. Had two strapping young dead men with her. So I made a better deal with the man himself right there."

"The fuck are you talking about?"

Drakesworth nodded at Leanna and shrugged. Another authority figure full of shit. No wonder the world was headed to Hell wrapped in butcher paper.

"How's it feel to get the ol' double-cross dildo right up your ass, bitch?" Richards started prancing like a rooster on Viagra. It made Leanna's guts implode.

"What are you—who were—Oh shit..."

Teena. Oh god. Please don't say—

"Yeah. Mommy's on her way right now to put you over her goddamn knee. I'd run if I were you."

"Aw, hell. Lee—" Mikey grabbed her shoulder, trying to talk some sense into her.

Leanna elbowed him in the gut and kicked him in the balls. His worrywart antics were gonna get them killed. *No more.* "Shut the fuck up, Mikey! All you do is bitch and whine and moan. Just shut your fucking mouth."

Without a word, Sharnell aimed her shotgun point blank at Leanna's chest. Leanna's eyes widened a bit. *Fuck, this is it.* But Mikey sprang up, pushed her out of the way and took the hit just as Sharnell fired, his chest torn open from the blast.

"Mikey!"

"Fuck, baby, I missed," Sharnell whined at Richards like she just spilled something on the kitchen floor. Drakesworth's goons closed in and took aim at Sharnell and Richards.

"Calm down fellas, she was just kiddin'," Richards chuckled.

"I am quite sure I told you not to dispatch them until I gave the official go ahead. That will be coming out of your bonus."

"Don't you talk to him like that, shithead. I'll blast you the fuck up, holmes."

"I do not know if you have noticed, but you are significantly outnumbered."

"Easy on the spice, baby," Richards cajoled Sharnell.

Leanna held Mikey in her arms, like she was cradling a big, bloody baby.

"I'm...killed, Lee. I'm—"

"Shhh, babe. Don't talk."

"You...gotta do two...things...for me..."

"What? What two things? Anything—"

"...You got to be...the best porno star the world's ever seen. You can do it. I know...you can."

Mikey wheezed painfully and coughed blood. Leanna laughed weakly through some tears.

"What's the second thing?"

"Kill...all of these...assholes for me, babe..."

Mikey died with a whimpering last breath, his head smacking the floor.

"Mikey! Mikey, wake up. I'm sorry I yelled at you, baby. You know how I get sometimes. Mikey! Wake up! I love you, okay? Are you happy now? I fucking love you!"

Richards laughed at Leanna. She decided right then and there it was the last time he'd laugh at anybody.

"We want the bitch. How much she worth to you, man?" Sharnell growled at Drakesworth.

"Less than nothing, now. Our transaction is complete, Leanna. Your business with these characters is your own. If you survive their ire, we can discuss renegotiating your deal."

"You fucking—" Leanna drew her gun and pulled her knife. Ready to die in the name of...*love*? Was that what was inside her right now?

What the fuck am I feeling right now?

And then, as if on cue, the Shakin' Bacon eighteen-wheeler smashed through the warehouse, taking out a bunch of Drakesworth's goons. Tires crushed flesh, bone, and business suit alike into a pulpy stew on the concrete floor of the facility.

"And that would be the mother, I assume," Drakesworth sighed.

A hail of gunfire erupted as the remaining squad of Drakesworth's men unleashed the fury of their MP40's directly as the Shakin's Bacon's metal skin. Bullet holes pierced its body everywhere, but no blood was drawn. No human movement could be seen from their vantage point. Drakesworth yelled for them to cease fire. A few long seconds later and all complied.

After what felt like an hour of silence, Teena simply hopped out of the driver's seat, completely unscathed. Just as she did, the back door of the trailer creaked open and five raging zombies filed out and sidled up next to Teena, convulsing and growling maniacally, ready to charge. Wallis, Ronnie, Lloyd Bob, J.D. Tyson, and even Good Old Vernon.

"J.D.? Lloyd Bob? What the fuck—" Richards looked legitimately baffled. Even he didn't know the whole gist of things. Leanna approved of that, if only fleetingly.

But then, Leanna saw *them*. Two ghosts from her past. One from long ago and one from just the other fucking day. "Ronnie? Oh fuck—Wallis?!"

"Who's that other guy?" Sharnell asked.

"Oh, that's Vernon. Long time, no see, Drake," Teena said and then went right into humming. The zombies charged, screaming unholy sounds. What was left of Drakesworth's goons opened fire once more and a huge battle rocked the facility, destroying any semblance of professionalism or decorum. Gun-toting gangsters and zombies collided with each other.

Sharnell, Richards, Leanna, and Drakesworth scattered and engaged in a wild shootout. None of them were fantastic shots. Add in the zombie element and everyone was popping off rounds willy-nilly hither and yon. Teena strolled through the carnage, eyes closed and humming casually, not worrying about much of anything. Bullets whizzed past her. A few perforated her flowing robes and gown. The shadows couldn't touch her here, it seemed. Nothing could.

A few of Drakesworth's goons managed to take out Good Old Dead Vernon with multiple bullets to the torso and head. His body convulsed like a convict in an electric chair, rotten blood escaping his body in jetting spurts. So much for his life as a revenant thrall to Teena. He most likely wasn't cut out for it. The other four zombies tore through a good chunk of the goons, ripping arms from shoulder sockets, legs from hip sockets, jaws from faces, and intestines from stomachs. It got to the point where it looked like a human jigsaw puzzle that would never be solved. One eviscerated goon vomited into his own stomach cavity just before fat and greedy Lloyd Bob ripped his throat out, plopped it in the guy's gut hole and chowed down on the makeshift human stew. Wallis and Ronnie seemed to find that hilarious and barked like demon seals at the sight. J.D. soon got taken out with errant shots to the head. He wheezed and sagged to the ground, leaking sputum and putrid blood from the top of his head and both ears. Lloyd Bob turned to his twice-destroyed partner and grabbed a chunk of his head and brain matter, eating it greedily as if the puking goon's tummy porridge had never even existed.

The few remaining goons had no time to regroup or celebrate J.D. and Vernon's defeat because Ronnie and Wallis, much more seasoned in the art of zombie attacks at this point, threw them around like rag dolls, snapping their necks and biting into their protective equipment like sharks trying to get into a closet full of canned veggies and pasta. Their squeals and screams as their blood went from inside their bodies to outside their bodies filled the warehouse and mixed with the sporadic gunfire and staccato trash talk and communication the remaining humans bandied about. Total confusion and chaos mixed with a heaping helping of involuntary end-of-life panic and regret.

~666~

Leanna and Drakesworth exchanged hasty shots with each other in the midst of all the chaos and carnage. They were both ensconced behind heaps of crates and boxes, using them as cover between bullet barrages.

"Your services are no longer required!" Drakesworth bellowed at her over barrels of meth.

"No fucking shit! I got my money, bitch. You ain't gonna leave here alive."

"You are without a doubt the most ungrateful, ignorant, stubborn—"

"Talk is cheap, Yaphet Kotto. Eat hot fucking lead!"

Leanna returned fire and as she ducked back down to her hiding place, Teena stood right in front of her. No words bandied about. Just a vicious staring contest of bad blood and resentment. This was it. She was here after all this time. She sneered at her mother, thinking hard of what to say as an opener. Many awful things came to mind but it had to be the *right* awful thing. What bothered her more was that Teena was smiling at her. Just *smiling*.

~666~

Lloyd Bob had found Drakesworth and his hiding place. He stared hungrily at the drug lord, anticipating a monstrous feast based on the size of such a man.

"You will not have me, beast! Come at me!"

Lloyd Bob let out a high-pitched squeal as he charged Drakesworth with gluttony in his dead eyes. BLAKOW! A bullet exploded Lloyd Bob's head and showered Drakesworth with hot, bony chunks of undead gore. Drakesworth dry heaved a few times and strained to see the source of his salvation. Ricky Richards pulled his revolver back to his face, smoking gun barrel just below his lips, and blew lightly.

"Always hated that fat fucking prick. Glad he's dead again. And you're welcome."

Drakesworth nodded hastily and wiped the sweat from his brow.

"Kill the girl and you can have whatever you want."

"Figured that. Better keep your head on a swivel. At least two more o' those fun police out there somewhere."

~666~

The staring contest from Hell soon ended as Leanna couldn't resist being the first to say something cruel. It was in her DNA.

"You got no business bein' alive," Leanna said, the blood draining from her face.

Teena ceased her humming and just smiled. "I would say the same for you."

"That's where you've come to, huh?"

"And a long time coming, don't you think?"

"How'd you find me?"

Teena pulled out the lock of blonde hair.

"So that hoodoo horseshit really works. You got a pin cushion dolly of me?"

"Too crude. An easy way out."

Leanna looked to the chaos of the carnage around them. A ravenous hellscape of death growing in scope by the second.

"This ain't no voodoo I ever heard of, Mama. This is somethin' else. This is what you been learnin' out there, away from me? Away from us?"

"Like I said, my child. Dolls and hair? Easy. I had to graduate to keep up with you."

"Ain't nothin' easy 'bout either one of us. You started all this shit and now I'm just playin' catch up."

"Is that how you see it, my child? I am so sorry."

"Get the fuck out of here."

Leanna slunk deeper into her cover spot behind the barrel. She didn't want to show any fear whatsoever, but just the very presence of Teena was different. Something was with her now. Something unsettling. And Leanna didn't like it one bit.

~666~

Richards met back up with Sharnell, their ammo running low.

"We got ourselves a deal with the honcho over there. Cha-ching!"

"That's my man," Sharnell gleamed, clearly proud of her man's trigger finger as well as his negotiation skills. From behind her, as they kissed, Wallis dropped from a ten-foot shipping crate and grabbed onto her neck, chewing into her skull, cracking and chomping it into a folded, brain perforating mess. Liquid, viscera, and chewed-up grey matter leaked out like the sloppy remnants of a broken soft serve machine.

"Baby! No!" Richards shot them both to pieces, mostly in the head, crying and wailing as he did so. Wallis and Sharnell amalgamated into a mixing bowl of flesh, blood, and gore as their twisted, entwined bodies flopped to the floor without a head in sight.

~666~

Meanwhile, a sweaty and mumbling Drakesworth pulled the pin on a grenade, intent on destroying Leanna and Teena with one fell swoop. As he tossed it, Ronnie jumped on him, fucking up his throw. The grenade landed in a pile of crates marked "CORPUS CHRISTI - FLAMMABLE" and exploded, starting a massive fire. Ronnie snacked on Drakesworth like a Mormon family of twelve at their first Chinese buffet, the kingpin screaming like a fainting goat as his skin ripped and shredded and his blood flowed like wine. Muscle and tissue tore and snapped like so much gristle with a litany of wet pops and crunches and squeaks. Drakesworth tried to grab onto a nearby crate and pull himself away from Ronnie, but there was no getting away from the grip of the hungry dead. His empire in flames all around him, Drakesworth kept screaming like a scared goat until he was no more.

~666~

Leanna and Teena paced around each other in a circle. The fire rising like sun-stoked daggers all around them. Leanna could feel the flames start to kiss her flesh. Soon they'd be doing a lot more than just that.

"You ain't gonna get no apologies from me," Leanna said.

"Sadly, I wasn't expecting any. Although I was hoping for one for Ronnie. And for Wallis."

Come again?

Teena charged her so quick and so fast, Leanna had no time to react. That level of vicious speed on her mother's part was unfathomable to Leanna. Teena grabbed her by the head while still holding onto the lock of hair.

"An apology. For Wallis."

~666~

Teena was in Leanna's mind now. It was even easier than she prepared for. This was what she had *really* hoped for. A definitive answer, a clear-cut explanation on Wallis's fate. She knew Leanna would never confess willingly, even though the evidence was stacked – *towered* – against her. She could see it all clearly now. That night. That accursed night of all nights.

Wallis was to surprise her at her own house. He had the dinner table set up all nice and pretty. Candles and fancy napkins and everything. He was humming the same odd tune Teena always hummed while he made a delicious spaghetti dinner. Noodles boiling, homemade sauce simmering in a big pot. As he stirred the sauce, he pulled out a black jewelry box and opened it, admiring the beautiful diamond engagement ring inside with a goofy smile.

So sweet. So unloved in his own life. And I failed him. I let her get him.

Leanna came in through the back door, all frowns and slutty go-go boots. Wallis was clearly intimidated and even frightened of Leanna. He tried to hide the ring and turned from her gaze.

"'Sup, retard."

"You're not...s-s'posed to be here. She's gonna be mad at you, L-Leanna."

"Oh, yeah? You gonna tell on me?"

"No..."

"Good."

She stomped over to the fridge and pulled out a six pack of beer.

"Hey, that's mine."

"Mine now."

Leanna popped the top on one and drank it down.

"Unless..."

She moved right up to him and played with his beard.

"Unless you wanna try to get 'em back."

Wallis's voice was a shaky mess now. "H-how? What do I gotta do?"

She lifted her leg and brushed her knee-high boot against his crotch up and down and then in a circular motion. His erection was near-instant.

"No. I—"

"What's the matter? Your eyes say no but your dick says yes."

"Y-your mom said you were bad."

"Did she?"

"Yup."

She dropped her leg and stepped back a bit.

"Did she also say that being bad can be really, really good? I bet she didn't. But it can."

She bit her lip playfully and moved in toward Wallis again.

"C'mon, take off your pants. Show me what she sees in you. It ain't for your sharp-ass wit. Show me that fucking shame boner you got going on in there."

"No. No. No means no, Leanna."

Leanna backed up with a disgusted frown. She folded her arms and stared at Wallis's crotch.

"W-what are you looking at?"

Leanna pointed to his waist. "Can I see your belt for a second, sweetie?"

I've seen enough. It's time.

~666~

Teena pulled back from Leanna, gasping from shock, yet still satisfied in some way with the outcome. Every nagging question had been fulfilled. Closure received. Now it was time to collect the bill.

"Did you even feel anything when you did it? For him? For me? For yourself, even? Anything?"

"Yeah, so what. I did it. And apparently it was okay with you 'cuz I never heard nothing otherwise."

"Murdering my lovers for attention. Not just one. All of them. There's no rule book for how far out past left field that is, my child."

"Stop calling me that, you fucking freak show. At least I saved Mikey from you."

Teena tried to reach out to her daughter, both arms extended. Leanna backed up with a snort.

"It was not for lack of trying, I assure you. He loved you. And look what it got him."

Teena enjoyed that dig at Leanna. It felt good to be on the giving end of such rancor for a change.

"Fuck you! You better not lay one fucking corpse-raising finger on him. You think that zombie shit is gonna make your life better? You can't change being a miserable, homewrecking cunt. Not fucking possible."

Leanna aimed her gun at Teena's head. Teena didn't start humming or anything. She could feel her children fading one by one. All she could sense now was Ronnie. Her last love. Not much longer now and she'd be all alone again, one way or another. She was ready for what was about to happen, regardless of the outcome.

~666~

On the other side of the warehouse, Richards sobbed uncontrollably as he shouted from his gut, shotgun at the ready.

Sharnell. Baby. I'll kill them all.

He was expecting Ronnie to pounce at any moment as he searched for the money in a mad haze. The fire was everywhere now. He had to find the cash before it went up in flames. This had all gone to Shitsville faster than he was ever prepared to anticipate. Sharnell was gone. The money, too, if he was being realistic at this point. But he had to keep looking. And that treacherous bitch was out there somewhere. She was responsible for all of this. That was enough to keep him going through this living hellscape. That last zombie needed tending to first. And who knew how many of these other fucks had been on the dust. It made him shiver and wretch.

"Come out, come out, come out, you unfortunate soul, you!" He flashed his shotgun all around, ready to blast Ronnie on a moment's notice. Ronnie came out alright, smack dab on top of Richards and chewed a chunk out of his neck with a sucking, slurping tear. Richards screamed, spun around and blasted Ronnie right in the face, splattering his head like a water balloon filled with blood and tumors. It even made a popping sound as it expanded to greet the rest of the warehouse with a sloppy red smooch. Richards bled like a whole litter of stuck pigs. He whimpered as he saw the briefcase of money. Just feet away.

I can make it. I can... fuckin'... make...it...

~666~

The flames were at their zenith all around, licking the ceiling in many spots. There weren't many safe places left to hide anymore. Soon, the whole warehouse would explode in a mammoth ball of flame. Smaller explosions rocked the facility here and there, threatening to trigger the big one. Teena and Leanna barely moved from their standoff.

"Unlike you though, I am here to apologize," Teena said as she put her hand on her heart.

"What?"

"For killing your father."

"You? Dad—"

"It was very much an accident, my dear."

"Fuck you! Fuck you! I—"

Teena wished she could just hold her daughter. Embrace her and tell her they could just go home now and try to make it work.

But it was too late. She could see the cancerous murderlust in Leanna's eyes. It wasn't going to go away as long as both of them were around.

The truth shall set you free. And me.

"The dust you love so much was in its early phases back then. Your father and I used it frequently. Until one day, he died while on it in the middle of an especially intense love-making session. I was heartbroken. And I didn't have the heart to tell you that I was responsible for your father's death. So I lied and said he had left us for another woman. I thought it would keep you sane. I had no idea how wrong I was."

"You fucking—" Leanna fired a shot into Teena's chest. It didn't even phase her. Teena lunged for Leanna and grabbed her by the throat. Leanna dropped her gun in a startled frenzy.

"Why...won't...you...just...fucking...die!" Leanna croaked in the frighteningly crushing grip of Teena's fingers.

It... It doesn't hurt. She must know why before it all goes dark.

"I died, too."

"What? You—"

"I took so much of the dust that I came back from the dead as a zombie. More than anyone else had ever taken. Much more than your father did. I was obsessed with it. It preserved me in my death, keeping me quite lifelike. No one knew, not even my lovers. Or you."

Leanna squirmed violently in her grasp.

"Bullets to the chest won't work, sweetheart."

Their struggle devolved into a messy fist fight and then a bizarre wrestling match, with Leanna trying to get away from Teena's smothering, crushing, boa constrictor-like grip as she rained down on her mother's face with wild haymakers.

"I forgive you, my baby. I forgive you."

"Get the fuck off of me!"

Leanna almost had a grasp on her gun and she reached with all her might. A gross popping sound echoed in the air as her shoulder dislocated right as she regained control of the firearm. She barely had a bead on Teena's forehead and fired without another thought.

"I forgive y—"

"Fuuuuck!" Leanna screamed as her shoulder screamed right back at her.

In that instant, as the bullet smacked into her skull, Teena knew right then why the shadows had followed her. Mocked her. Prodded her. How could she be so blind to it?

The dead look after their own, Tee-Tee.

She thought she could see Hector out there, beyond the veil. He seemed happy. Maybe it wasn't so bad after all if he was there now.

Teena went limp, a veritable robot switching off one last time. The blonde lock of hair fell from her hand.

"You know what? I forgive you, too," Leanna said, much more softly and reverently than she thought she was capable of sounding. She scrambled to her feet and eventually found Richards, clutching the briefcase for dear life, and parked in a growing pool of his own blood. "That's mine, buddy."

Richards could barely speak; he was plum near out of blood. And good old, basic wherewithal.

"What...about...my...tip?"

Leanna aimed with one squinted eye and the tip of her tongue sticking out of her mouth and emptied the rest of her gun's clip into the vicinity of his face. His features shredded into pulpy, crimson nothingness with each bullet hit. A blenderized tomato if she ever saw one. His body shuddered a few times before all went still on his person.

"That enough of a tip for ya?"

Groans and moans rose up all around her. In the flames she could see Drakesworth's goons coming back as zombies.

That motherfucker gave out the dust like it was Halloween.

There was no time to shoot it out. The place was about to go nuclear and there weren't enough bullets in the building to fix this fuckup. She leaned up against a concrete pillar and inhaled and exhaled a few times.

Now or never.

Leanna slammed her shoulder as hard as she could three times until her should POPPED back into place. Her eyes leaked with tears and she struggled to stay on two feet as she was forced to deal with such slobberknocking pain. It was even more agonizing than the actual dislocation.

As she cursed her existence and swore into the blazing chaos of her situation, she saw Drakesworth rise as one of the undead. Another satisfied customer of Love Potion #666. Leanna was annoyed she had just thought of a name for the stuff. Talk about a late bloomer.

"Fuck this shit."

~666~

Leanna smashed through a plate glass window clutching the briefcase with a bloody hand. A monstrous, whooshing fireball followed right behind her.

As she ran to the parking lot, bags of cash and dust in hand, the building exploded in an even bigger fireball of narcotics and undead-fueled obliteration. *Meth inferno, baby.* Leanna spotted the sleek BMW roadster parked further away than any other car. The one Mikey was all atwitter about. She pulled out a set of car keys and smiled painfully, pressing the lock door button on the key fob. Drakesworth's key fob. The BMW squeaked to her that it belonged to said key fob. She staggered as fast as her bruised and battered legs and her gimp shoulder would allow to her brand-new BMW.

Signing bonus, bitch!

Speeding out of the parking lot, Leanna forced herself to look back at the blazing warehouse and swore she saw Mikey through a shattered, flame-kissed window. Staring at her with dead yet wistful eyes. She let out a rebel yell of defiance and hit the gas. That would make the ghosts go away for sure.

~666~

She felt like she'd been driving for days. States bled into each other. She had only stopped to refuel a few times using cold, hard (and hard won) cash and even that level of necessity felt like a few stops too many. Not even knowing what state she was in but assuming it was Texas, Leanna sped recklessly down the interstate, the stuffed case of cash and dust next to her in the passenger seat. A bottle of vodka also sat by it, waiting to be noticed. She scanned the entire gamut of radio stations, listening for something. Nothing. Just commercials, static, and bad pop music. No news of what happened at all. Odd. But it wasn't going to get in the way of Leanna's non-stop celebration grand prix.

For Mikey.

"Here's to ya, Rundgren!"

Leanna took a swig of the vodka, cackled maniacally, and pushed the gas pedal all the way down with a bloody, bruised bare foot. The cops were the least of her problems. She knew how to deal with them. Something else nagged at her from the back of her mind. She had to get home. A place she swore she'd never go back to. But it was all fucked. Mikey was gone. But then so was Richards. And her mother. *Maybe Killford's out of the picture, too?* She hoped at least Jiman was still around.

Only one fucking way to find out.

FORTY-FIVE...

Drakesworth's car careened into Teena's driveway and smashed into a huge potted plant, coming to a crashing halt. Leanna hated that potted plant anyway. Teena named it Ferdinand. What a fucking stupid name for a plant, let alone a person. Leanna flung the driver's door open. Wads of cash and pouches of dust fell out in a pile. Some of the bills clung to her bloody legs.

Home sweet home.

For a split second, she thought about keeping the house as it was. The last and only memory she'd have of her mother. It was just a split second, though.

She walked right through the front door like she owned the place.

And at this point she did.

~666~

She flopped onto the couch in the front room, a satisfied smile plastered across her face. She opened the bag and dumped out the dust pouches and stacks of cash, rubbing them all over her like she was taking a greed bath.

After a bit, she pulled out her phone and called someone.

Goddamn voicemail.

"Hey. I'm back. You ain't gonna believe this here story. I got the best business proposition you're ever gonna get. We can corner the market around here. Meet me at the Cluck Shack in an hour. I gotta get—"

A grumble and a growl and a groan stopped Leanna cold. It most definitely came from inside the house...

You've gotta be fucking kidding me...

She opened her eyes and looked up to see a rotting, bearded walking corpse leaning over the couch and hovering just a foot or so above her face. Patchwork flesh, tattered suit. A burial suit. A corpse fresh from the grave.

"Who the fuck—"

Then she realized something. Something awful and horrible that should have been heartwarming. Life-affirming. In another life.

"...Dad?"

Then another desiccated figure leaned into her field of vision. Tall and gangly. Mangled dreadlocks. Missing an abdomen.

"Oh fuck, Jim—"

The zombies squawked and vomited black crud all over her face before swooping down and chomping on her neck.

~666~

Somewhere out in the deep woods there was a clearing. The unmarked grave Teena had visited before she departed was now empty, mounds of dirt piled on either side. Scrapes and claw marks covered a ripped-open cheap wooden casket. The huge grave marker lay flat on the ground. Like it was placed there.

~666~

Leanna screamed a bloody, gurgling scream as Derek Forsythe and Jiman's dust-driven reanimated corpses devoured her lickety-fucking-split. As Jiman consumed each bite of her, the masticated flesh popped out of his frayed esophagus and onto the floor, creating a pile of freshly chewed chunks with each wet plop. Leanna squeezed a stack of cash with a death grip, hoping it would save her life somehow, as dumb as it sounded. As her father bit deep into her throat, she desperately grabbed her larynx, trying to keep it in place. Her labored screams turned to squirts and gurgles as she was completely torn apart and eaten alive, bite-by-bite.

Her last lucid thought was of Mikey, believe it or not. She sure couldn't.

~666~

As Mr. Forsythe and Jiman finished eating Leanna, Zeb appeared at the front door, peering in. He was bandaged up and bruised real good. J.D. and Lloyd Bob had worked him over something stiff. At his age, it was astounding he even survived such a beating. He shook his head and snickered as he leaned back out and headed down the porch stairs.

"Well shoot. Guess it takes all kinds nowadays. Poor gal."

He scooped up a couple loose hundred-dollar bills strewn about the gravel driveway. A few of them had splotches of blood on it. Maybe Leanna's. Maybe someone else's. He licked his thumb and tried to clean them off like an overzealous mother wiping snack gunk off their kid's face. As he pocketed the cash, Zeb hummed the same weird tune Teena used to hum. Almost as if he taught it to her.

Or she taught it to him.

Zeb turned his hum to a whistle and he caught someone out of the corner of his eye approaching. He turned to meet their gaze and a slow smile formed out of his whistling.

"Oh, hey there, Miss Mirabelle. Miss Teena ain't come back yet but you can stay awhile if you like. I'm sure she won't mind. Just need to clean up a little inside if'n you don't mind. Other than that, not much else goin' on 'round here, I reckon."

EPILOGUE

Leanna's death dream went something like this...

Laid out on a plaid chaise lounge in her dressing room, Leanna and Mikey were naked and feeding each other infinite doses of the dust. Love Potion #666. She felt in love. She felt loved. She was lost in his soft, buttery face and baby blue eyes as she felt him fill her slowly. Considerately. Like they were floating on a cloud of pink, cottony orgasms. All three of them. Her, Mikey, and his perfectly proportioned cock.

They were happy.

It was almost time to be back on set, though. They were starring in their own adult film epic together. Finally. Living the dream, just like Mikey wanted. Just like she wanted, too, to be honest. *Tits & Pits: A Texas Fuck Story*. A title Mikey had fantasized about for years. She was Tits, he was Pits. Lusty private eyes who stumble their way into a Texas oil fortune through murder, deceit, and sex.

She knew it wouldn't last. *Couldn't* last. This would end, too. But it felt like it could go on forever. It had been going on forever. Right? Mikey seemed so happy. He had to be real. The conversations were real. They talked about how much they hated Corpus Christi and how glad they were to be in Vegas. She confessed to him her love of vintage polka music and he told her his secret fear of short women, those just under four feet thereabouts. She laughed and he sulked, awash in vulnerability.

Maybe this was more than just a dream. She wasn't sure about a higher power. She never took the time to think about it. Maybe now was a good time.

She wanted to just concentrate on Mikey. His tight pecs. Perfectly tanned skin. Not too dark, not too light. His toned ass. Just rubbing up against him triggered a series of orgasms that made her stutter and convulse. No cock necessary at this point. Or could that just be her brain being chewed out of her cracked skull out there? But the dust made her feel *so good*. The love. The ecstasy. She was born to feel like this. To have this forever.

But too much was too much, even in a dream. They eventually sniffed all the dust they had right as they were being called to set. Leanna felt her body convulse hard one last time, her insides shutting down. Was this how her dad felt when he died? What was *his* death dream like? Did he think of Teena?

Of course she had to think of her mother now.

Of all the fucking...

And then she was just plain dead.

THE END

RECOMMENDED WATCH LIST

(AKA Fifteen Movies That Inspired *Love Potion #666*)

THE BAD SEED (1956)

THE BIG BIRD CAGE (1972)

SWITCHBLADE SISTERS (1975)

STREET TRASH (1987)

THE SERPENT AND THE RAINBOW (1988)

WILD AT HEART (1990)

BRAINDEAD (AKA DEAD ALIVE) (1992)

TRUE ROMANCE (1993)

KALIFORNIA (1993)

NATURAL BORN KILLERS (1994)

FROM DUSK TILL DAWN (1996)

THE WAY OF THE GUN (2000)

2LDK (2003)

HOBO WITH A SHOTGUN (2011)

SAVAGES (2012)

CINEMATIC POTIONS OF LOVE:
A FRIENDSHIP FORGED BY CHARACTER(S)
(OR A BRIEF HISTORY OF *LOVE POTION #666)*
A SHORT ESSAY BY THE AUTHOR

First and foremost, it must be stated up front that the characters of Leanna, Teena, Mikey, Ronnie, and Wallis are the creations of my best friend, Chad Farmer. They originally appeared in the short screenplay *Dead of Night*; a segment written by Chad for a feature film anthology entitled *Lurk: A Horror Anthology.*

Chad and I met in film school in Orlando, Florida in 2008. I heard him talking to a few other people about movies he enjoyed watching recently and it was music to my ears. *Independent. Foreign. Horror. Gangster. Martial Arts.* I had to approach this guy. He knew what was up.

Long story short, we came to be pretty good friends throughout the rest of our stint at film school and when the time came to go our separate ways, we agreed to meet up later in the year to shoot a feature film together in Oregon at the behest of a former friend who shall remain nameless.

Needless to say, that former friend was not much of a producer and the shoot quickly spiraled into chaos, infighting, and indecision. We shot the whole thing (even some reshoots the following year) but it was such a terrible film. Neil Breen-level bad but without the unintentional laughs. Just boring. We thought we knew everything right out of film school, and it turned out we knew jack shit.

A few years later, we went back to the drawing board after a few trips to some film festivals just as avid movie buffs. We decided we'd start simple and make a short film this time. You know, what we should have done from the beginning. Lo and behold, we got accepted into a handful of film fests with our first film, *Late Submission*. A heartwarming little tale of two disgruntled filmmakers who take a festival runner and his family hostage. Oh, and it was a silent film shot on Super 8mm.

We've made a handful of shorts together since, all playing at fests around the world (there was even a screening in the Amazon rainforest).

But one thing kept coming back to me.

Dead of Night. Specifically, the characters from Dead of Night.

Homicidal Leanna. Vengeful Teena. Horny Mikey. Duplicitous Ronnie. Poor Wallis.

I loved them. Chad has a knack for making hilariously fucked up characters that still manage to remain endearing and somehow sympathetic.

The long and short of *Dead of Night* is that Teena and Leanna, a most warped mother/daughter pairing, face off against one another amid a sea of shitty male lovers and confront their hatred for each other with Teena finally getting the upper hand thanks to her being able to raise their lovers from the dead as voodoo zombies. A short twenty-page script that mostly takes place deep in the woods in the (you guessed it) dead of night. Simple dimple.

I wanted more from those characters and with Chad's blessing, I started work on a feature screenplay that took those characters out of the woods and into the world at large. What the hell would that be like? Well, you're holding it in your hot little hands right now. After winning a few awards and placing at film fests and competitions (including FilmQuest and Buffalo Dreams Fantastic Film Fest) the script kind of just sat there. Too expensive for me to make on my own, too raunchy and mean to get picked up by Hollywood, it languished.

Until, that is, I went to the Scares That Care Convention in 2019 and discovered the world of indie publishing. I should have known such a thing existed. If it worked like that for indie film, why not for indie books? I felt like such an idiot. I could have been writing for the indie genre market for years now.

At that point, I knew what to do with the screenplay for *Love Potion #666*. After several drafts and tweaks and beefing up the narrow prose of a screenplay, here is the final result. Make no mistake, those five characters were born in Chad's short script from all those years ago, but everything that transpires in this book is completely and wholly a creation of yours truly.

It's a weird evolution of a story but it's a testament to how much fun these characters are and how much I love collaborating with Chad and his warped mind. I'd write a follow-up in a flash, but well... You see...

I...think I've said too much.

I hope you enjoyed *Love Potion #666* and if there's something in there you weren't a fan of, just blame Chad.

I do.

P.S.: It's 2024 now and I am most definitely writing a sequel entitled *Love Poison #9* on the heels of releasing the second edition of Love Potion #666. Buckle up, that one's going to be crazy fucking ride. I really want to do a shootout at the Cluck Shack sandwiched between car chases. For now, though, enjoy this first blast of action and horror and if you end up savoring these characters like I do, hit me up and we can talk about action and horror movies into the wee hours of the night. I mean, a guy can dream, can't he?

ABOUT THE AUTHOR

Nathan is a writer and filmmaker who enjoys the cheerfully nihilistic side of life and fiction. *Love Potion #666* is his debut novel. His short story collection *The Comfy-Cozy Nihilist: A Handbook of Dark Fiction* was published by GenreBlast Books in 2023. He has published short stories with Grinning Skull Press, Timber Ghost Press, D&T Publishing, and Terror Tract Publishing. He has a few more books in various stages of undress and hopes to half-ass them to completion sooner rather than later.

He is also an audiobook narrator and the director of the GenreBlast Film Festival at the Alamo Drafthouse Cinema in Winchester, VA. It was recently named one of the Top 50 Genre Fests in the World by MovieMaker Magazine, so it must be a swell time. He produced the feature film adaptation of Grindhouse Press' *Worst Laid Plans* along with its editor, Samantha Kolesnik.

He loves Asian cinema, independent pro-wrestling, Warren Zevon, and a good spicy ramen. He lives just outside of Richmond, VA with his wife Mary and their two daughters, Georgie and Charleigh. Currently on the hunt for a new house and a puppy. In that order.

His podcast, The Reel '96 Podcast, is a deep dive into every single movie from 1996. You can find it wherever podcasts are available. You can follow him on Twitter and Instagram @loogenhausen and on TikTok at nathan.d.ludwig

ABOUT GENREBLAST BOOKS

GenreBlast Books was founded by Nathan D. Ludwig and Chad Farmer to highlight genre fiction that revels in the weird, the absurd, the transgressive, the violent, and the subversive. Stories without limits or agendas. We publish what we want when we want.

You can find us online through the @GenreBlast social media accounts and at www.genreblastbooks.com.

Please leave a review for this book on Amazon and Goodreads. It helps authors and publishers more than you know. Thank you.

Milton Keynes UK
Ingram Content Group UK Ltd.
UKHW011120180424
441376UK00004B/82

9 798218 384760